MW01196038

The Nicholas Book

A Legend of Santa Claus

William Chad Newsom

ISBN: 978-0-692-80281-6

Published by Family Lore Publishing
An imprint of Cross and Quill Media
Liberty, NC

www.crossandquillmedia.com/familylorepublishing

Cover art and design by Richard Svensson.
Visit him online at http://fiverr.com/loneanimator

"*The Nicholas Book* is **a delightful tale**, with a lovable family, in an interesting town. The mystery makes the book **a page-turner**, and the discovery of the answers to the questions posed regarding Santa **keep one reading to the last page**. Light a fire, pour a mug of hot chocolate, and enjoy this Christmas Story."

Nancy Carpentier Brown, Social Media Director, The American Chesterton Society, contributing editor of *Gilbert* magazine, and author of the *Father Brown Reader* series, *A Study Guide for G.K. Chesterton's St. Francis of Assisi, How Far Is It to Bethlehem: The Plays and Poetry of Frances Chesterton*, and *The Woman Who Was Chesterton*, a biography of Chesterton's wife, Frances.

Other Reader Reviews of *The Nicholas Book*

"Since I downloaded the book, I have never had a moment of peace with my niece who **wants me to read and reread the book for her all the time** even when it's not bed time. The book actually brought back memories. It's **a wonderfully written book**, one that every family needs to have for this Christmas."

"My family downloaded and read this while traveling this weekend and what can I say? My 5 year old SAT THROUGH THE WHOLE THING and LOVED IT! He like short books and stories but **he LOVED THIS ONE!** I love how it brings out the real meaning of Christmas yet still allows the whimsy of Santa Claus. **Awesome book that will DEFINITELY be a new family Christmas Tradition**!!! Great author! Look forward to more from him in the future too!"

"**A great read** for the child who needs more than just a 'yes' or 'no' to the great Santa question – and, perhaps more importantly, to the parent who wishes for some of that magic of Christmas to continue past the classic 'Santa' years. **A pleasure to read**."

"This book is **an amazing and unique telling of the legend of St Nicholas**. It weaves together **a rich and deep history**, a **captivating narrative**, and **a positively magical message**. If you've ever wondered how to explain Santa Claus to yourself or your children this book is for you."

"...**a fun read**... the story is a good one and **well written**...."

Reader Reviews of William Chad Newsom's
The Crown of Fire

"A stirring read for young people."

"...very well researched and blends fact with fiction to make an exciting adventure story..."

"Reading *The Crown of Fire* was well worth it...I was captivated by the dialogue Newsom powerfully crafted..."

"...well written and chock full of fascinating history and well researched facts."

"perfect reading material, especially the spiritual aspect of the book...[we're] racing through the book and gaining a good bit of Church history at the same time!"

"...grabs the reader's attention on page one, and then weaves an action-filled story through to the final page. Drawing from ancient records, William Newsom paints a vivid picture of life during the early days of the Christian church. Once into the story, it is hard to put it down...The accuracy of historical events in Newsom's writing makes this an enthralling way to learn history."

"Let yourself be transported to a world far different than our own through the writings of Newsom."

To Grace, William, Nathanael, Abigail, Kaitlyn,
and any who might follow.

Some of the pictures of Father Christmas in our world make him look only funny and jolly. But now that the children actually stood looking at him they didn't find it quite like that. He was so big, and so glad, and so real, that they all became quite still. They felt very glad, but also solemn.

C. S. Lewis, *The Lion, the Witch and the Wardrobe*

What has happened to me has been the very reverse of what appears to be the experience of most of my friends. Instead of dwindling to a point, Santa Claus has grown larger and larger in my life until he fills almost the whole of it.

G. K. Chesterton

Contents

Part I: The Quest

Prologue

The scholar sat at a table in the Library, writing furiously, sweat dripping occasionally from the sides of his bald head, or behind his thick glasses. Some obsession drove him today, and he scribbled on. What was this strange sense of foreboding? Something was about to happen, of that he was certain. In an hour, he was slated to lecture to a local club, The Anti-Superstition League, right there in the library, on a subject chosen by the sponsoring group: "Scientific Proof of Atheism" (the title always gave him the giggles). But now his thoughts were constantly wandering to the door, as if he were waiting for someone; someone he had never met. But he couldn't account for the feeling, so he merely loosened his red and black tie and took a deep breath. On scratched his pencil.

Seven and a half minutes later, a thunder burst in his heart, and he involuntarily stood, scattering his papers, his pencil still in his hand. He walked rapidly to a nearby window, peering outside desperately, his midnight-black eyes groping for something, anything that might explain this strange feeling of destiny. Words formed in his mind, so distinct from himself that he had to force himself to listen: *Today, today. Something you have long sought draws near. Today.*

His muscles were tight, his face so stretched in wild eagerness that a young child walking by outside, happening to glance up at the window and the face, ran quickly away in fright. His hands clenched tighter than a vise, he responded in his mind to the words he had heard: *today. A thousand towns and countless years and it is finally here. They are coming.*

The pencil snapped in his hand, startling the librarian.

Chapter One

Candy Apples

As the pencil snapped, two children walked out the door of their house just outside the southern edge of town, shouting goodbyes to their mother and siblings inside. They walked through Mom's beautiful little kitchen garden, even now resplendent with snowdrops and winter honeysuckle, and the fresh, heady smell of oregano and sorrel. They walked leisurely and joyfully, talking rapidly, laughing at everything, even bursting into occasional song, for this was the first day of the Christmas holidays. They looked at everything, land and sky, Heavens and Earth, and all looked new and bright, as if they were seeing it all for the first time; the world seemed like a new garden, freshly-fallen from her Maker's lips.

They headed northward on Star Street, into the heart of the town where they lived. It was called Bethlehem, a common enough name for an American town in 1959. But this town took its name seriously, making Christmas a public and civic celebration, not just a privately-observed holiday. Streets, shops, and restaurants often took Christmas-inspired names. And it had been a town tradition for over a hundred years for a community choir, made up from the church choirs all over town, to put on a holiday concert a couple of days before Christmas. And as you might guess, their closing song was always *O Little Town of Bethlehem*. Christmas was a way of life here.

As the children walked, their thickly-wrapped bodies got warmer, but their naked faces got colder, and redder; they even saw themselves in the window of the Woolworth's, looking like cherry-headed gingerbread children; but they didn't care, laughing at this as at everything else.

After about twenty minutes, they had reached the northern edge of town. There on the right, sprawling over several paved acres, was their destination: Wiseman's Department Store. Inside, a plastic wonderland met their eyes: snow, candy canes, reindeer, a Christmas castle and throne, and, best of all, Santa Claus himself. There he was—larger than life, a mountain of red fur and white ermine; the poetic twinkle in his eye almost visible, even at that distance; a merry chuckle beneath his billowing beard.

"It's really him!" whispered ten-year-old Joshua Kirk, one of our two heroes.

"I know," was the awed answer of his twin sister, Rachel.

They would be coming back Friday night with the rest of their family; but on this Day of Days, a day that, half-unconsciously, they looked forward to as much or more than Christmas Day itself, they couldn't resist coming by for their first glimpse of Magic—real Magic—seated on his Christmas throne. It was a four-year's-running tradition, and had become as much a part of the holiday season as Scrooge, or Christmas trees, or even the Manger itself.

For several minutes, they gazed on in wonder and, perhaps, not a little adoration, watching the children wait in turn for their moment on that Numinous Lap. Anyone who remembers that childhood wonder will know how they felt, to be so close to the One whose magic was strong enough to fly reindeer, squeeze rotundity down chimneys, and visit every Christian household in a single night. Their skin tingled with excitement: they could feel the enchantment all around them. They heard Santa send forth one of his great and famous laughs, and as he did so, saw him turn his eyes upon them. Both gave a little gasp, as Santa raised his hand to them in greeting. They timidly returned the wave.

Joshua and Rachel stood thus for a quarter-hour, just watching, and listening. Even in the middle of a weekday, the bustle around the throne was as busy as the court of any king. Courtiers, in the form of Wiseman's employees, dressed as elves, walked among the crowds, helping to keep the line moving. Joshua and Rachel believed firmly that Wiseman's Santa was the one and only, but they were under no illusions about the "elves;" though they accepted gratefully enough candy canes the elves offered to onlookers, and to the kids in line. Of these there were quite a few, some guided by parents, some on their own, the line stretching back beyond the roped pathway almost to the edges of the Toy Department. Two dressed-to-the-hilt soldiers, in Napoleonic uniforms, but looking more like toy soldiers, kept guard by the throne. It was a scene of hectic enchantment.

The magical fire never dimmed in their hearts; but presently, perhaps fearing that overexposure would somehow snap the spell, Rachel and Joshua sighed, kicked a bit of fake snow off their boots, and walked around to the other side of the Christmas kingdom. A rather loud rendition of "Santa Claus is Coming to Town" was playing over a store loudspeaker, and the clamor of the children and shoppers was a bit overwhelming. The store had set up a small concession stand on the marches of Santa's domain. Food and drink seemed anti-climactic; but this was a day of celebration, so they wandered over toward the little booth, hoping for some popcorn or a candy bar. They dug into their pockets for nickels as they approached.

"Uh-oh," said Joshua, glancing up.

"What is it?"

"Look." He pointed to the concession stand, which Rachel now saw was manned by a boy they recognized at once.

"It's Lou!" said Joshua with a roll of his eyes.

Lou Nyten, a boy in Joshua and Rachel's class at school, advertised himself as a very modern, progressive kid. Lou had taken up a somewhat singular hobby: find a person who believed in something he thought silly (like Fairies, or Easter Bunnies, or God), and then, with all the ferocity of a Roman gladiator, impale such belief bubbles with his very up-to-date intellectual sword. For this reason—and this reason only—he attended Sunday School each week; for it made him giggle like a toddler to explain to hapless little second graders (after class, of course) that "modern science had proven that Noah's flood could *never* have happened!" He drank the ensuing bewilderment like Kool-Aid.

"Yes, it's Lou," agreed Rachel. "We'll pick up something to eat somewhere else."

"But he's waving us to come over," said Joshua. "What do we do? I know—I'll challenge him to single combat, proving on his body that Noah was a real guy." He grinned at his sister.

"No, that won't be necessary," said Rachel, grinning back. "And don't be rude. You know how you are."

Joshua cocked an eyebrow at her. "How am I?"

"You love arguing with Lou." In fact, the banter between Lou and Joshua had become legendary, the playground counterpart to the Lincoln-Douglas debates of a hundred years before. Joshua enjoyed it, mainly because nearly all the spectators were on his side, though in the opinion of a teacher who overheard one such exchange, Joshua was beginning to develop a primitive, though real, debating skill.

"Not true," replied Joshua. "I don't love *arguing* with Lou. I only love *winning* the arguments. Not that I know what it's like *not* to win."

"Don't be arrogant. But I suppose we'd better find out what he wants." They walked toward the concession stand. Rachel noticed a flyer tacked to the counter, advertising a lecture at the library later that day. The photograph of the lecturer gave her a shiver of repulsion. The man looked positively beastly to her. Not that he was ugly, for despite his bald head and thick glasses, he had a noble and handsome face. But there was something in the eyes, and in the expression, that revolted her, though she wasn't sure what it was. She saw that the lecture was sponsored by the Anti-Superstition League, and she nodded knowingly, for Lou's father was the president of the ASL.

"Well, if it isn't the two Kirk kids," said Lou as the siblings came over. "Hi, Joshua, hi Rachel."

"Hello, Lou," said Rachel, attempting a smile.

"What is it, Lou?" said Joshua, without even the hint of a smile. "Let me guess: you just read a magazine article on how science now proves that giraffes aren't real?"

"Ha! That's a good one," said Lou, slapping his thigh in mirth.

4

"How'd you get a job here?" Joshua asked. "Aren't you a little young?"

"My Dad knows Mr. Wiseman. He lets me work a few hours here and there, after school, or on the weekends."

"Weird," said Joshua.

"What?"

"Mr. Wiseman goes to our church. What's your Dad doing hanging around a Christian?"

"Joshua," whispered Rachel, in a tone of rebuke.

"No, now, don't be like that," said Lou. "I want to be friends."

"Friends?" said Joshua. "What do you mean by that?"

"I sense that you doubt me. Here: my pledge of good faith," said Lou, picking up two gorgeous candy apples and holding them out toward the two children.

"How much?" said Joshua, eyeing the apples a bit greedily.

"On the house; or, to be more precise, on me."

Joshua was not even inclined to *buy* anything from Lou; *taking* something he'd offered for free felt like signing in blood to join some dark conspiracy.

"What's the catch?" Joshua asked.

"No catch. I just thought you looked hungry." His arms were still extended, and he had an almost-pleasant sort of smile on his face.

Rachel glanced around the store, trying to look uninterested. The line had dwindled and Santa was rising from his great chair. Then Joshua spoke.

"I'll bet they're poisoned or something. We'll probably turn into atheists if we eat them."

"Joshua!" whispered Rachel, a bit more urgently. Joshua could be hard to rein in once he got started.

Lou laughed again. "They're just regular candy apples. Scout's honor!"

"Like *you* would ever be in the Scouts!" said Joshua.

5

"Now you're just being mean. But my offer stands. You want them or not?"

"Okay, thanks." Rachel spoke quickly, wanting to defuse whatever firecracker retort was brewing in her brother's brain. "You'll have to forgive Joshua for being suspicious. But—no offense—it is a little surprising, coming from...well, from you." She took a bite of the apple, and Joshua, reluctantly, followed her example.

Lou grinned. "Maybe so. Maybe I just want to learn to be nicer. Like you guys."

"These are...really good." said Joshua, still with hesitation. "Er...thanks, Lou."

"You're welcome." He paused for a moment, apparently enjoying the apples more than they did. Then he leaned in and spoke somewhat quieter. "Listen, I meant what I said about the candy apples being free. But, um...*if* you wanted to do something in return, I'll make it easy on you."

"Uh-oh, here it comes," said Joshua. "I knew there was a catch." He glanced around, as if he expected Lou's cohorts to be hiding, ready to spring on them. Santa was walking away from his chair.

"No catch," said Lou again, glancing at the Christmas throne. Then he began to speak more quickly, urgently. "I just want to show you something."

"What?"

"Just a minute. Hey, Larry!" He turned and asked his boss if he could have a quick break. "Now," he said, turning back to the two children, "follow me."

"What for?" said Joshua.

"I want to show you something."

"What is it?"

His voice sunk to whisper-level. "Something secret. Something worth knowing."

Chapter Two

Something Worth Knowing

Normally, Joshua and Rachel would never even consider doing something that Lou suggested. But, perhaps on the mannerly conviction that, after all, he *had* given them the candy apples—or, perhaps, as Joshua later suggested, under some spell wrought by the candy apples themselves—they reluctantly agreed. Then again, it may have been, as Rachel believed, that Lou's promise of secret knowledge was more alluring to them than they fully realized. But even as they followed him away from the concession stand, they felt that they were making a mistake.

Walking quickly, Lou led them around to the back of the Christmas castle, where there was a little hallway. Several doors led out of this hallway, but Lou bypassed these, jogging to the end of the passage where he took a door that led out of the store. Then he led the children to the left. A line of bushes followed the wall to the corner; near the corner, Lou suddenly crouched down behind the bushes, and got on his knees. Then, just as suddenly, he jumped up with a yelp.

"Snake! There's a snake!" he squealed, falling backwards over the bush and onto the sidewalk.

Rachel and Joshua looked behind the bush. Rachel laughed. "It's just a little garter snake, Lou. They're harmless." She reached down and picked it up, showing it to Lou.

"Hey, get that thing away from me!" He edged back against the wall.

Rachel set the small snake down where she'd picked it up from, and it slithered into a small hole in the earth. "It's probably looking for a place to hibernate before it gets too cold."

"Never mind that," said Lou, who still had a clammy sort of look on his face. He took a deep breath.

"Was *that* what you wanted us to see?" asked Joshua with a hint of a smirk.

"No," said Lou. "Just a minute." With that, he reached down, and quickly, but almost silently, wrenched a loose brick out from the wall at about waist level. He knelt down and peered through the gap he'd made.

"Good, he's not here yet." He stood up. "I found this last year," he said, motioning to them. "Hurry. Look through here."

Greatly doubting the wisdom of their choice, the children bent down behind the bushes, one on either side of the brickless gap, and peered, with one eye (which was all they could fit, with both of them looking at once) into the hole. They both gasped at the same time.

They were looking into a dressing room, and there, just a few feet away from them, was Santa Claus himself. He had just walked into the room. But what happened next hit them like a punch in the stomach. Santa sat down heavily in front of a mirror, breathed deeply, stretched his arms, yawned, and then, to the horror of Rachel and Joshua, *he took his beard off.*

They were so stunned by this that they couldn't move. The beard was attached to the great red cap, and so it came off at the same time, revealing a patch of thick brown hair and a face hairless except for a pencil-thin mustache. Then, another man came in the room, a man in a suit. He was wearing a name tag with the Wiseman's store logo. He and "Santa" began talking. The children never afterward remembered what they had talked about, except that, in the course of the conversation, the department store man had several times called "Santa" by the name of Hank.

Rachel and Joshua stood, silently. Neither of them looked at Lou. They simply did not know what to say.

"I'm...sorry to have to do this," said Lou, his brow furrowed with concern, but his mouth still bearing an irrepressible smile, "but I thought it was important to, uh...well, to tell you the truth, see. That *ain't* Santa in there."

"But then..." began Joshua, before falling silent. His voice had none of the combative confidence it had held earlier.

"I know this is hard," said Lou, sticking his hands in his pockets, "but we all have to grow up sometime. Santa's not real; he's *never* been real."

"That's not true!" shouted Joshua.

Lou raised his hands and cocked his head. "Hey, don't get mad at me. I'm not the one in there lying to kids. You can be as superstitious as you want. I just give you the proof. But if you *want* to know, science has shown that—"

"That's enough, Lou. We don't want to talk to you anymore," said Rachel. She looked into her brother's face with eyes that instantly renewed his courage. Then she turned back to Lou, who could not conceal an ugly smirk of delight at puncturing, as he thought, yet another balloon of childish belief.

"Lou, you sure like to talk about 'proof' and 'science.' Well, my uncle is a scientist—an astronomer—and he believes in a lot of the things *you* say are just bunk. But that doesn't matter. Because the truth is, you don't care about science at all. All you care about is making other people unhappy. There's plenty of proof for *that*."

Lou started to speak, but Rachel cut him off.

"Lou, you can say what you like, I don't care. Just don't say it anywhere near us. Ever again." She tossed the remaining half of her candy apple in a trash barrel that stood at the corner of the building. Joshua followed her example, and the two children walked away from the store.

Lou stood watching them for a moment, then, with a somewhat confused look on his face, turned to go back inside. The confusion quickly turned to anger, though, as he inwardly defended himself against Rachel's words. *It's not true,* he said to himself. *I do care about science and proof. That's the only reason I bother with stupid little kids like them. Well, I'll show them.* But how? He turned, gazing intently at the disappearing children. Then a vague, half-formed idea took shape in his head. With fierce determination and no clear plan, he began walking quickly, following Rachel and Joshua as they trudged through the streets of the little town. He would have to stop at a payphone and call Larry to explain why he'd had to leave suddenly, of course. But he was confident he could come up with something believable to say.

Chapter Three

The Quest

Some time passed before Joshua or Rachel found any words to say. The cold air seemed to freeze all speech on their lips. It was as if their eyes were opened, and they knew...well they weren't sure just what they knew. But in a different way, they felt completely blinded. They walked southward, back down Star Street, passing the Frankincense Theater on their left, where *Ben Hur* was playing. Near the center of town, they ducked into Shep's Diner, a place they often visited with their Mother while running errands. Just crossing the threshold and feeling the heat within brought a measure of comfort, small but real.

They ordered root beers and sat down in a corner booth, as far away as possible from the three other customers in the Diner during that pre-lunch hour. They took off their heavy coats and hats, for they were hot and red-faced after their walk. They felt cooler uncloaked, Joshua in well-worn dungarees and a sweater, Rachel in a turtleneck and jumper.

Even after sitting, silence ruled for a while as they sipped their sodas. As so often happened, Joshua broke the silence.

"Rachel, I feel like...I don't know. Like..."

"I know. I was thinking about it just now. You feel like you just watched a TV program where somebody took a camera up to Heaven and found it was empty."

Joshua nodded. "Yeah. Exactly."

"I know," said his sister again, glancing out at the Christmas shoppers passing by the large glass window. They seemed so happy. Did they know what the children knew? Was the whole thing just a big fat grownup conspiracy? Was *everyone* lying to them?

"I've always just laughed at Lou," said Joshua. "He's never bothered me before. Remember that time he said he'd found a bone from the missing link between monkeys and humans? He tried to tell everybody he'd proven Evolution was true."

Rachel smiled. "Yeah. Turned out to be a bone from Mrs. Whillikers' old cat."

"But this time," said Joshua, "he was right. Santa Claus is... well, I mean, the man in the store was not him."

"That's true," said Rachel. "And it really bothered me. We've been coming to that store for years, to see Santa. This was one of my favorite days of the year. Now Lou's destroyed all that."

An angry look passed over Joshua's face as he answered. "Yeah, he's good at destroying stuff."

"But I've been thinking about it on the way over," said Rachel. "Look here: remember that movie we saw on TV last year: *Miracle on 34th Street*?"

"Yeah. About how the real Santa Claus came to New York, but some people didn't believe it was really him."

"Right! Well, remember how it started? Macy's Department Store hired a man to play Santa in their parade."

Joshua's eyes brightened, seeing where his sister was going with this. "Yeah, I remember!"

"And," she continued, "some of the kids thought that he was the real Santa. But even though he wasn't, that didn't mean there was no Santa. In fact, the real Santa was much closer than they thought!"

"Yep," said Joshua. "So maybe all the stores use...actors, or something, to play the part of Santa, just...just for fun, I guess."

"And to help sell toys." She pondered for a minute. "And that makes sense, you know. Remember a year or two ago, when we heard Bing Crosby on the radio, singing that song about Santa Claus?"

"Yeah, 'Santa Claus is Coming to Town.'"

"Yes, but remember what Dad said? We asked him if Santa could really see us when we're sleeping, and if he always knew whether we were being bad or good?"

"Yeah, and Dad said, *no way, only God knows what's going on all the time. Santa is not God,* he said."

"Yes, I remember that, too. But the point is, if Santa can't be everywhere at once, like God can, then the stores would *have* to get actors to dress like Santa."

"That's right," said Joshua. "Like Dad said, *Santa's not God.*"

Rachel looked troubled. "Maybe that's part of the problem. Do you think...do you think we've been treating Santa like he *is* God?"

Joshua squirmed in his seat, and looked bothered. "I hope not. But...well, maybe we have, a little."

"I know I think about Santa a lot more than Jesus during Christmas."

"Yeah, me too." Joshua's voice was very quiet, now. "Why do we do that?"

"I think I know," said Rachel. "We believe in God, but we can't see Him. Santa is someone we *can* see...at least, that's what we've always thought. But you know, Mom and Dad warned us about this. I mean, about not making such a big deal about Santa Claus and toys. And I've noticed that they don't talk about Santa, or not very much."

"Yeah," said her brother, "and I remember a few times I asked Dad some questions I had about Santa."

"What did he say?"

"Not much, really. He was kind of...mysterious. Talked a lot about legends and magic, and stuff like that. But it didn't really help much."

"Hmm, that's interesting." She sipped her root beer and pondered deep matters before continuing. "Come to think of it, I can't really remember a time when Dad *or* Mom have ever come right out and said Santa Claus was real."

"Really?" said Joshua, as he turned the matter over in his mind. "Yeah, I think you're right. But what does that mean? Do you think they do believe in Santa Claus? Or *anything* magical?"

Rachel didn't like the implications of the question. *Magic* was an important word in their house. "Some things I'm sure of," she said, and her voice took on a tone to match the words. "They've told us every day of our lives that the Bible is true and the stories of Jesus are real. But they haven't said much about Santa Claus. Almost everything I know about Santa I got from friends at school, or books, or movies, or Christmas songs."

"So then..." Joshua didn't want to say what he was thinking. "Then, *is* Santa Claus real?"

"Of course," said Rachel, a little too quickly. But her mind was starting to spin, and it was making her feel a bit dizzy. "At least...I'm pretty sure he is." Silence held them until half-melted ice cubes rested alone in their now frostless mugs. The Shep's Diner banner, tied to a pole outside, began to flutter wildly in a new wind from the north. Joshua watched it blankly, saying nothing. Then Rachel sighed, but it was a sigh of sudden resolution. She turned determined eyes toward her brother.

"Listen, Joshua. There *are* answers to our questions, somewhere." She paused for a moment, remembering something. "You know Eliza Driver from school? I found her crying in the hallway the other day. She was upset because she'd made a 'B' on her math quiz."

"Why would she cry about that?"

"Her parents have really scared her with talk about how she won't get any presents from Santa if she's bad, or if she lets her grades slip. I tried to tell her Santa isn't like that, but she wouldn't listen. She *couldn't* believe me, I think. I know that a lot of the things kids say about Santa are just rot. He's *not* God, and he can't see us when we're sleeping, and all that. And I never believed that stuff about how we wouldn't get presents if we're bad."

"No, me either," said Joshua. "But...*why* don't we believe that?"

"What do you mean?'

"Okay, I mean, Mom and Dad don't say much about Santa, right? And everyone else believes they'll get coal in their stockings if they're bad. So why don't we believe that too?"

"Because Mom and Dad aren't like that," said Rachel, and it felt to her as if she'd just uttered the most profound thing she'd ever thought in her life. "They give presents at Christmas because...well, because they're Christians, and because they're happy, and they like doing it. Because *they're* that way, I just never could believe Santa was any different."

"Yeah, you're right. So, then, a lot of the stories about Santa are silly, or just wrong. But does that mean Santa himself is not real?"

"No, it doesn't." She pointlessly sipped her empty mug. "All right, think about this: what if I said that George Washington was the Holy Roman Emperor?"

"You'd be wrong."

"Yes, but would that mean Washington himself was not real?"

"No."

"So then, Santa might still be real...or he might not. I don't know. But like I said, *somebody* knows. There are answers to our questions. And I think we should find out the truth. Let's spend our Christmas holiday this year finding those answers."

Despite his worries, and the generally depressing nature of their day so far, this suggestion fired Joshua's imagination. "Yeah, kind of like an Adventure. Or a Quest."

"Yes," agreed his sister. "It is a Quest."

Chapter Four

Lady Quack

It was a quarter past eleven. They had the rest of the day ahead of them, for Dad and Mom were both out: Dad at work, and Mom doing some Christmas shopping. "That means we're on our own," said Joshua, for of course the children's first thought had been to talk to their parents. Instead, they would find as much as they could on their own, and talk it over with Mom and Dad that evening.

"But where do we begin?" asked Rachel.

"No idea. But look—Christmas is everywhere around town right now: decorations, shopping, music. Let's walk around town, and just, I don't know, talk and think. We're bound to come up with something."

This seemed sensible, so they left the Diner and took a left, walking down the sidewalk of Stable Road. Then they crossed back over Star Street, heading west. Neither spoke as they trudged heavily down the sidewalk, their breath ghosting out in front of them in the frosty air. That air was also alive with sounds: laughter of Christmas shoppers, car horns honking, the chatter of conversation, the scuffle of boots and shoes on the sidewalk. And one other sound: one they could hear, somewhat distantly, but could not yet see whence it came: a single handbell, being rung with a fierce constancy that bordered on wildness. It took a few minutes for this sound to get close enough for them to notice, but when they did, they both stopped in their tracks.

"Uh-oh," said Joshua, looking at his twin sister. "Lady Quack."

"Don't call her that," said Rachel. "I didn't realize we were so close to Herod's."

17

The crowd ahead parted, and Joshua could see the sidewalk in front of Herod's

General Store. "There she is. Look: let's go ahead and cross the street here. Maybe she hasn't seen us yet."

Rachel considered this idea. "Lady Quack" as she was known to most children around town, was really Ms. Gloria Track, and she used to be a teacher at the Bethlehem Elementary School. She had been Rachel, Joshua, and Lou's third grade teacher, a little over two years ago. Lou had loved her, for she had been a key figure, along with Lou's father, in the Anti-Superstition League, and she had often supported Lou's efforts to attack the faith of his classmates. As a teacher, she couldn't say too much, back in those days when the Christian faith was still openly acknowledged in American educational institutions, but she did what she could by means of winks, sly looks, and allusive suggestions. Rachel and Joshua had not liked her much; but Lou was delirious with joy those first few months of the school year, for Ms. Track was the first teacher he'd ever had who was not a Christian.

Then, without warning, the dream was over: Ms. Track suddenly quit her teaching job, a few weeks before Christmas. No one seemed to know why, but there were many mysterious rumors, the most common of which was that Ms. Track had gone crazy in the head. Lou had been devastated, all the more so because Ms. Track's replacement had been a steely-eyed Presbyterian gentleman who was not in the least afraid of Lou's challenges. No one saw Ms. Track for a few days; then, she had simply reappeared one Wednesday in front of Herod's General Store as a Salvation Army volunteer. That Christmas, and the two Christmases since then, she had been there every day the store was opened, ringing her bell and wishing passersby a Merry Christmas, and (most strangely), saying, "God bless you" to those who left money in her donation can. This whole affair was all the more striking since, as an officer in the Anti-Superstition League, Ms. Track had never before celebrated Christmas. And that was the other thing: not only had she resigned as a teacher, but she had also resigned her position and membership in the ASL.

She had developed quite a reputation for eccentricity in the two years since her resignation. The kids at school had come up with various nicknames for her: "Off Track" was an early favorite, but "Lady Quack" had stuck. The nicknames had come, not so much from Ms. Track's rumored insanity, but from her eccentric mannerisms: she was a bit wild-eyed, talked fast and constantly, had a rather crazy laugh, and a tendency to get off track in conversation (part of the reason for one of her nicknames). But there was actually a method in her madness, as the children had been warned by their Mother, who knew Ms. Track, and her comments were always on point, even if they didn't seem to be.

Joshua and Rachel found all this disconcerting enough; but they also wanted to avoid Lady Quack because she had a special talent for trapping people in long, unwanted conversations. She would talk for hours on end if something didn't interrupt her. Rachel had once spent three quarters of an hour talking to her about, of all things, horseshoes (Lady Quack was an ardent student and collector of lucky charms), causing Rachel to miss her piano lesson. But Mom had given Rachel and Joshua a strict rule: "always speak to her, and with the utmost courtesy; and always put at least a little money in when you pass her by. She may not have been the best teacher, but she remembers you children fondly."

This of course made the choice before the children doubly hard: should they disobey Mom, and selfishly cross over to the other side of the road, avoiding the talkative, crazy Lady Quack? Or should they obey, and consequently show a bit of kindness to a lonely woman? If they did what they both knew was the right thing, their Quest might have to be delayed, possibly for quite some time, for Lady Quack was notoriously unstoppable once she started talking.

Rachel spoke first. "No, you know what Mom says. Come on. Get out a nickel and let's go."

Joshua sighed and shook his head slightly as he dug in his pocket for a coin. "I guess you're right. Well, let's get it over with."

They walked on toward the General Store. In front of the shop was a little red Salvation Army donation can manned by the Ringer of the Bell. She appeared to be a very young woman with straight, fine, black hair, and piercing black eyes. She had at one time been quite lovely, and still seemed so from a distance. But the bright red Santa Claus hat perched jauntily but somewhat crookedly on her head distracted the eye from whatever beauty remained; that, and her curious necklace, strung with crosses, clovers, coins, and other such lucky items. It was also apparent from closer range that her natural beauty suffered somewhat from neglect: her fine hair was wild and uncombed, her clothes ill-fitting, wrinkled, and just a bit threadbare. This striking figure of beauty and negligence glanced up at the children, and her eyes and smile went wide with recognition and happiness. "Joshua! Rachel! My dear children!"

"Well, here we go," said Joshua with resignation in his voice. "Let's go talk to Lady Quack."

"Merry Christmas, my delightful little ones, Merry Christmas!"

"Merry Christmas, L—er, Ms. Track," said Joshua.

"Merry Christmas, Ms. Track," said Rachel.

"It is so, so, so good to see you! Thank you sir! God bless you!" This last was spoken to a gentleman who had just placed a handful of quarters in her can. Ms. Track never stopped ringing the bell, even while she talked, and this quickly became a maddening irritant to both children.

"You too," said Joshua, making a move toward the can to drop in his nickel, hoping by this to transition into an exit line. But he was not quick enough. Ms. Track shook him warmly by the hand before he could deposit the coin.

"I hope your parents are well!" said Ms. Track.

"I'm sorry?" said Rachel, and "Excuse me?" said Joshua, for neither of them had quite heard what she said over the ringing of the bell.

"I said," continued Ms. Track in a louder voice (though the effort made her unconsciously start ringing the bell even more vigorously, so the effect was quite lost), "I hope your parents are well."

"They're fine," said Rachel, who caught the words this time. "Thanks for asking."

"What's that?" said Ms. Track.

"I said, they're fine, thanks for asking," repeated Rachel in a louder voice.

"You've been fasting?" asked Ms. Track, somewhat puzzled.

"Not fasting! Asking! I said my parents are fine!" Rachel cupped her hands to her mouth as she half-yelled these words, wincing at the throbbing sound of the bell, which was, she now noticed, both bigger and louder than the average Salvation Army bell.

Ms. Track looked confused and a little distracted. "What about the wine? What wine?"

"No, not wine," Rachel was indeed shouting now and starting to attract attention. "*Fine!* They're fine. My parents are well."

"Oh, the bell? Thank you, I'm quite fond of it myself," said Ms. Track. "I bought it on my own, rather than using those dinky bells they normally issue to volunteers. Gets more attention, you know. But Rachel, you really ought to stick to one question at a time in a conversation, dear girl. I was asking about your parents!" She chuckled and shook her head with a smile. "But never mind. Merry Christmas, ladies!" she added to a couple of passersby: evidently only those who actually clinked a coin in the coffer got a "God Bless You!".

"Do you know," she continued to the children, "I saw little Larry Winston earlier today? Not so little anymore, though! He was one of the cutest little boys in the class: not so cute as Bill Mulligan, of course, but hardly one child in a thousand has those enormous crystal-blue eyes like Bill, you know, so it's probably not fair to even include him in the accounting."

For the next fifteen minutes, the children were treated to a discourse on the relative cuteness of every boy in every class Ms. Track had ever taught. And all to the constant, throbbing, head-pounding ringing of the bell. "Jack rather reminded me of James Wilkins," continued Ms. Track, "though James always spoiled his potential cuteness with that constant scowl. God bless you sir! Merry Christmas! Kind of like Lou Nyten, really, who might have been cute except he always had that arrogant little smirk on his face that quite ruined his features. I rather liked Lou at the time, but I don't think I would care for his type much if I...if I were teaching now." She fell into a contemplative silence for a moment, though her tireless arm kept swinging the bell. Joshua made a move toward the donation can once more, but the sudden movement seemed to bring Ms. Track back to life.

"Lou Nyten," she said so suddenly that Joshua was startled and dropped his nickel, "reminds me quite a bit of myself at a young age. Always eager to be on the cutting edge of modern thought, you know? Likes nothing better than to shock innocent minds with radical new ideas. Haven't seen him in a while. I hope he's grown out of it."

"He hasn't," said Joshua, as he retrieved his nickel from the sidewalk.

"Yes, he was just up to his same old tricks earlier this morning," added Rachel.

"He's been sick?" said Ms. Track.

"No, he's up to his old *tricks!*" shouted Joshua. "He's still the same as always."

"Really? That's too bad," said their old teacher. "You know, it wasn't so long ago that I would have agreed with Lou. But that was before... well, that was before." Again, she stopped talking for a moment, and Joshua got his coin out once more. He reached out again for the can, but Ms. Track started talking, and he pulled back his hand with a sigh. He wanted to save the dropping of the coin as the transition to his move out of here.

"So what are you two up to today? I've seen lots of kids about this morning. School's not out already is it? Where *does* the time go? But where are you two heading, dear children?"

"Well," began Rachel, "we're not exactly sure."

"I see," said Ms. Track, "too many fun things to choose from, eh? Or..." She paused, and looked hard at the children, as if something had just occurred to her. "Wait a minute here: you look bothered, my little ones. This doesn't have anything to do with whatever it was Lou said to you, does it?"

Joshua was startled by this shrewd guess, but Rachel remembered that Ms. Track always had a gift for that sort of insight; and, despite a warning glance from her brother, she decided to tell her old teacher what had happened. And so she did, telling the story (with many interruptions and misunderstandings under the domination of the insane bell) of how Lou had disenchanted them from their beliefs regarding the Wiseman's Santa Claus. Rachel ended her account with, "and so we're out to find out the truth about Santa Claus. We just don't know where to begin." Rachel and Joshua had expected either a laugh at their silliness (but then, that would have been more consistent with the Old Ms. Track), or perhaps a word of sympathy. Instead, Ms. Track's bell-hand dropped suddenly to her side, and the smile disappeared from her face. The silence after the mad bell ringing struck the children like a blast of thunder.

"Santa Claus, yes, I see. Santa Claus. Indeed. *Ghosts,*" she added, unexpectedly, in a louder voice that made both children jump. Then her voice changed, taking on a high, almost falsetto tone, as if she were talking in her sleep, or to a baby. She was not looking at the children now, but gazing off at some distant point. "Yes, I know. It was a ghost. But who? Who? William of Leyland, that's who. That's what Old Cass said. And then he showed me the book. The Old Page. The Old Page. And Saint Nicholas. I don't care what they say. *I'm* not the crazy one, no indeed. And now I've lost all my little children. I *can't* go back and teach, not now. I led them all astray. It was William of Leyland that did it. That's what Old Cass said." She closed her eyes and a whimper of pain or sorrow escaped her tormented lips.

The children could make nothing of these wild words, nor did most of the names she mentioned (except Saint Nicholas of course) mean anything to them; and both were becoming a bit frightened at her condition, feeling certain that the rumors of Ms. Track's insanity were not exaggerated after all. The retired teacher stood so long with her eyes closed that the children were just about to slip away, skipping the donation for fear the clinking of the coins should startle her into some mania. But just before they moved, she opened her eyes, and let out a deep sigh. She looked at them and smiled, and seemed quite herself again, whatever that might mean.

"Father Lewis," she said then. "You should go see Father Lewis."

The children were still puzzled, but here at least was a name they recognized. "Father Lewis?" said Joshua. "You mean Father Lewis of Saint Augustine Church?"

"Yes, that was it," answered Ms. Track. "Saint Augustine. He can help you."

"That's a good idea," said Rachel. "Father Lewis is an old friend of our Dad's. Maybe we can stop by his church and talk to him."

"He's not there. God bless you, ma'am! Merry Christmas" She seemed to lose her train of thought, for she said nothing further.

"He's not there?" asked Rachel. How do you know?"

"Father Lewis comes by here every day and puts some money in my can, and chats for a few minutes. He's a good listener. I like him. But he said he was going to the library today."

"Oh. Well, maybe we can find him there, then. Thank you."

"Wait—I want to give you something." She took off her heavy necklace and rummaged around among its many pendants. Finally she located a tiny money purse and opened it, removing something small and thin.

"Here," she said. "Take this. Perhaps it will bring you good luck in your search. It certainly never brought *me* much luck, for the gnomes—or maybe it was the leprechauns this time—ruined my corn with this coin hanging right there around my scarecrow's neck. But sometimes a lucky piece is meant for some and not others. I hope it will help you. But promise me this: after you've finished your search, please give this coin to Father Lewis—Father Lewis, and no one else. Okay?"

It was a grimy, faded little coin, but very possibly made of gold. It bore Latin inscriptions on both sides and the image of what appeared to be a Roman Emperor. Right through the middle of the coin was a small hole, as if the coin had once been nailed up, like Captain Ahab's doubloon.

"A Roman coin," said Rachel. "That's very kind of you. But are you sure you don't want to keep it? It might be valuable."

"Oh, it is!" she said with intense feeling. "But I want you to have it, to help you on your Quest. But remember to give it to Father

Lewis when your Quest is achieved. Merry Christmas, Rachel and Joshua."

"Well, thank you, then, and Merry Christmas, Ms. Track." The children dropped their nickels in the donation can, and Joshua pocketed the much more valuable gold coin. Then Ms. Track took their hands in hers and held them in a tight squeeze for some time. Joshua thought she looked like she was going to cry. But she didn't, and she released them, waving to them and inviting them to come see her again. They promised they would do so, and, with confused feelings, but a destination in mind at last, they continued on their Quest, leaving Lady Quack behind them, ringing the bell as if her life depended on it.

Chapter Five

"There are No Dead"

The children were quiet and thoughtful as they continued west on Stable Road, heading toward the end of town. Both felt that they understood "Lady Quack" a little better now; and though the thought of enduring that incessant bell was a bit much (and though it would be some time before their headaches went away), they both inwardly resolved to visit her again when they could. They had silently made another decision as well: to take Ms. Track's advice and seek out Father Lewis.

The last building on the right, at the very western edge of town, was the library. It was called the Bethlehem Public Library, and indeed it was currently funded by the City; but the great building itself, the gigantic tapestries and paintings on the walls, the beautiful auditorium and ornate conference rooms inside, and at least two thirds of the books, had all been paid for by a very large gift by an anonymous donor over a hundred years before. It was a large stone building, and Rachel sometimes thought it looked a bit like a church. They ascended the thirty-three steps that led to the massive oak doors, and entered.

They looked everywhere for Father Lewis, and even asked the librarian for assistance. But she had not seen him, which, she was quick to add, didn't mean that he wasn't here. It was a big library, after all. Finally, though, they gave up, and Joshua suggested that as long as they were there, they ought to see what wisdom they might be able to find in books.

Rachel agreed, and they looked around, wondering where to begin. On a bulletin board on the right, Rachel saw another of the Anti-Superstition League flyers with the dreadful-looking man on it. Noting the time, she observed that the lecture was probably about over. And in fact, as her eyes turned to the entrance to the little auditorium in the left-hand corner, she saw him: a man with a bald head and a red and black tie, carrying a briefcase, with an overcoat hung over one arm. He looked even stranger in person, so Rachel hurriedly led her brother in the other direction, thinking to herself that the man looked like just the sort of person Lou and his father would like.

But the lecturer had seen her as well. He had been about to leave the library when he glanced up and saw the two children. His black eyes narrowed as he watched them. Then he smiled. *They are here,* he thought to himself. Some people who knew the eccentric scholar were often taken aback by his sudden flashes of intuition, things he just seemed to know, for no apparent reason. But he felt confidence in these inner promptings, and followed them faithfully. The children were looking in the card catalog in the middle of the room. Instead of leaving, the bald man sat down at a nearby table, took out a book, and pretended to read it.

For the next hour, Rachel and Joshua tried everything they could think of: history, folklore, children's books, poetry, novels. They found lots of books about Santa Claus, legends, poems, and books about the man known to history as Saint Nicholas, but nothing to really answer their questions.

They were sitting at a table, each reading a different book, and thinking that the Quest was going nowhere fast. Joshua tossed several dead-end books onto a red couch beside their table. Suddenly, they were startled by an auctioneer-speed whisper just behind them.

"What's this? Kids at the Library during the Christmas holidays? Have you taken leave of your senses?"

They jumped, startled, and turned around. Then they had to stifle their laughter. For there, behind them, wearing a broad smile and a clerical collar, was Father Lewis of St. Augustine Church.

"Father Lewis!" said Joshua, a bit too loudly.

"Not so loud, Joshua," said the priest, taking a seat at their table. He was tall and dark, but wore a short white beard that neatly matched his clerical collar. He was an old friend of the family, and had been a mentor to the children's father in his younger years. Though the Kirk family had never attended Father Lewis' church, they had remained close friends, and Dad had the utmost respect for the priest, about whom he often said, "there's more about him than you might think." Father Lewis was widely respected, but he had a knack for getting in trouble, too—though never the sort of trouble that impugned his character in any way. It just seemed that the priest's superiors had never been quite pleased with him. Dad had never exactly told the children what the problem was, but he had hinted that Father Lewis "preached too much St. Paul to ever rise very far in the church hierarchy." The children had always loved him, for he was quick with a joke, and had a way of always saying things that surprised them. He was something of a legendary figure in the town, too, some saying that he worked miracles, others that his dreams foretold the future. He never said much about any of this, however, except to chuckle quietly at some of the stories.

"So, what brings you two here on the first day of the holidays?" he asked.

"We were looking for you, actually," said Joshua with a big grin. "But we looked all over the library and couldn't find you."

"I attended a lecture that ended a short while ago. Then I got caught up in a conversation—more of an informal debate, really—with one of the sponsors."

"You didn't attend that awful atheism lecture, did you?" asked Rachel, remembering the scary face on the poster.

"I did," said the priest, "but only to keep up with the devices of the Enemy, so to speak. And to see if perhaps God would give any occasion for me to say a word or two on behalf of the Truth. But how on earth did you know I would be here?"

"Lady Qu—I mean, Ms. Track," said Joshua. "She told us you could help us with a little problem we have."

"I see. And what problem is that?"

"We're on a Quest," said Joshua, "to find out the truth about Santa Claus."

"Ah, Santa Claus," said Father Lewis. "And since you are looking for the 'truth' about that worthy gentleman, I assume you have now come to question whatever it is you've been told in the past?"

"Well, let's just say we're wondering about some things," said Rachel.

"Are you not content with what your father and mother have taught you?"

"It's not that," Rachel said. "In fact, we were just talking about it earlier: Dad's always been a bit mysterious when he talks about Santa Claus."

"Which is not often," said Joshua. "But we found out something today, and...well, now we're more curious than usual." They told him about their encounter with Lou, and their conversation with Ms. Track. Father Lewis knew the child, and frowned with disapproval as they told their tale.

"Yes, you're quite right about Lou, I'm afraid," he said. "I think perhaps he *wants* to be scientific, at least as he imperfectly understands the term; but this good desire is usually trumped by a stronger desire to be a spoilsport. Some of the children from my church have had run-ins with him. I shouldn't bother too much about it, if I were you, but consider this: to the extent that you were deceived about the department store Santa Claus, I think you can be grateful to Lou, even if his motives were poisonous. Truth is terribly important, you know."

This made both the children stop and think. "Yes, I suppose you're right," said Rachel. "And while we're talking about truth, maybe you can help us."

"If I can be of any assistance to you, God's gift of life to me this day will not have been in vain."

She smiled. "Thanks. We trust you, and I know you would never lie to us. So I'm just going to ask this straight out: is Santa Claus a real person?"

The priest did not blink, or flinch, or hesitate. "Yes, of course he is a real person."

The children smiled at each other, for the priest's tinderbox words had kindled a spark of hope. They both suspected there was more to this answer than they knew, but they were also certain that Father Lewis would never tell them an untruth.

Joshua groped for more clarity "'Is'...or 'was'?"

"Is." The priest's eyes locked onto Joshua's as he said this.

"Okay, then. Next question: are all the stories about Santa Claus true? I mean the stories about reindeer, and the North Pole, and all that."

"Are *all* the stories true? Certainly not," said the priest. "Some of them were only invented recently. But beyond the advertisements, and the movies, and the songs, there is a bit of history, and a good many legends, about old Saint Nicholas. A legend, you know, is a story that may be true, or not; often it seems wild, or improbable, a tall tale. But no story was ever as wild as the world itself; and if there are truly tall men, then there can be true tall tales."

"Then are any of the stories true?" asked Joshua.

"I'll tell you this much," said Father Lewis. "Chesterton was right when he said that it is much easier to *do* legendary things than it is to *be* the kind of man people make legends about."

"Saint Nicholas was a church bishop, wasn't he?" said Rachel.

"Yes, born in the fourth century."

"But is Saint Nick alive today?" asked Joshua.

"Of course," said Father Lewis, and, once again, he spoke with no hesitation, no sly looks.

"But didn't he die then?" said the boy, his whispered words chapped with knowledge-thirst.

"Well, now, there are two schools of thought on that question," said Father Lewis with a look of mystery in his eyes. "But suppose he did die? You've heard of the Communion of the Saints, yes?"

"Sure," said Joshua, for he and his sister had been carefully brought up. "That's the whole Church, past, present, and future, right?"

"Right. Well, now, Jesus Himself says that God is not the God of the dead, but of the living. In that mysterious world to which we go after death, everyone is alive. Heaven is not strewn with corpses: the saints there rest, but do not sleep; they are alive, but their life is spiritual, not physical. Until the Resurrection, when their bodies will be raised, they live on, but in a different way than we do now. If we saw them here, no doubt we'd think they were ghosts. But as a great writer once said, one can't be a ghost in one's own country."

"I think I understand," said Rachel. "And the dead in Christ are with us, here and now, in some mysterious way."

"Especially when we gather in Church," said Father Lewis, "but perhaps at other times as well. As Saint Augustine wrote, 'there are no dead.' The Cloud of Witnesses surrounds us. Just what they *do* as they surround us has not been revealed. But why couldn't some of them work among us, invisibly, perhaps, even if we don't realize who they are?"

"And are you saying that is what Saint Nicholas does?"

"Oh, that's more than I know," he replied. "But I'll tell you what. If you really want to know more about this legendary man, I can help you."

Rachel smiled. "Thanks," she said.

"Well, now, have you children ever heard of The Old Page Bookshop, out on the eastern edge of town?"

Both children looked at each other, a little wild-eyed. Both of them realized at the same moment that this must have been what Ms. Track meant: "The Old Page" she had said. Perhaps now they would find out why she had sent them to Father Lewis. "Sure," said Joshua. "But I've never seen it."

"You can't see it from the road," said the priest. "The owner, who is a friend of mine, doesn't advertise, and is not out to get rich through his little shop. Very few visit him there, and that suits him just fine."

Joshua considered his next words carefully. "A kid at school says that old bookshop is...haunted." And again, he and Rachel remembered Ms. Track's words: "Ghosts," she had said.

"Yes, I've heard that, too," said Rachel. "Is it true?"

Father Lewis leaned in closer, and spoke more quietly. "You know what? I think it is."

No one spoke for a while. Father Lewis' words would have startled, and perhaps alarmed, some grownups. But Rachel and Joshua were not startled; only fascinated. They waited to hear what he would say next.

"Haunted it is, then," he said. "But there is no reason for *you* to be afraid."

Joshua and Rachel held a quick and silent council through meaningful glances, and made up their minds at once. "Okay, we'll go," said Rachel.

Father Lewis was pleased by this. "Excellent." He gave them directions for finding the shop, and then said, "Now, when you go there, you must talk to the owner, Ezra Tome. Tell him you want to look at *The Nicholas Book*. He'll show you where to find it."

"*The Nicholas Book*," said Joshua. "Will that book answer our questions?"

"Some of them, anyway. Though it may also raise new questions. But either way, I believe it will help."

"How do you know about it?" asked Rachel.

"Oh, it's been there for some years," said Father Lewis. "I have read it a number of times, though not for several Christmases, now. It was for this book that Ms. Track sent you to me."

"But it's a bookstore," said Joshua. "Will *The Nicholas Book* still be there?"

"Yes," said Father Lewis, mysteriously. "Yes, it will still be there. I am certain of that. Now, off you go. And let me know how it all turns out."

"You're not going with us?"

"No, I have some visiting to do, and I must work on my sermon for Sunday. But I will see you again, soon. Oh, and tell Ezra I sent you, all right?"

The children thanked him, and headed for the doors, while Father Lewis went back to the theology section, where he planned to do some reading.

As the children walked out the door, something stirred behind the red couch where they'd been sitting. Then a head peeked over the top of it. It was Lou. The boy had followed them to Shep's Diner, where he had waited outside, pretending to window-shop at nearby stores, until they came out. Then, he'd trailed them to the Library. Lou had followed them with nothing more than a vague idea of revenge in his mind: revenge for what Rachel had said to him at Wiseman's Department Store. But he had no clear idea at first what he wanted to do. Now, having heard everything the children and the priest had said, including their talk about him, he was angrier than ever—but he had a plan at last. He left the library, and followed them down the busy street.

After Lou left, the bald-headed scholar with the red and black tie rose from his chair, put a book in his briefcase, and walked outside. He could just see Joshua and Rachel as they reached the bottom of the steps, Lou close behind them, trying not to be seen. He kept his eye on them as they headed east, down Stable Road; then, he followed them. He had been waiting for this moment for many years.

Part II: The Book

Chapter Six

The Hooded Man

A light rain was falling, and the sky withdrew behind a curtain of grey. Wispy clouds descended upon the town, floating overhead like so many formless ghosts. Joshua and Rachel hurried down Stable Road, the Quest driving them on, thirsty for truth, impatient for knowledge. But patience is better for truth-seekers, and in their urgency they failed to heed the age-old advice to Watch Where They Were Going. This resulted in the kind of thing that usually happens when age-old advice is ignored: in this case, a collision. Joshua and Rachel ran headlong into a shopper emerging from a sidewalk store. The shopper staggered back into the doorway, flailing, and caught the door frame, but lost his packages. Joshua spun off the shopper like a billiard ball, and then knocked into his sister, sending her spinning in like fashion. Indeed, a severe encounter with the sidewalk seemed certain, but both children suddenly found themselves suspended in mid-air, their plummet to earth mysteriously halted.

They hung side by side above the pavement for a few moments like cabled Christmas pageant angels, catching their breath, before they regained sufficient presence of mind to turn their heads upward. A hooded man held them in the air, by the scruff of their jackets. At first that was all they noticed. Then they saw his face, and their mouths uncorked like the pop of a wine bottle—a perfect image of their speechless surprise, for the hooded man was none other than their very own father.

They smiled when they saw him, both because they were relieved to have escaped a nasty meeting with the pavement, and because he himself wore a wide and contagious grin. Joseph Kirk was a tall man, and stout, as they say, but not so very fat; and he had a beard. The beard was not all that thick or long, but it often seemed so, being very out of fashion in those days of Eisenhower and Ward Cleaver. He wore a tie and jacket, all covered by a red rain coat, the hood of which shielded his head against the still-falling rain. His eyes twinkled with merriment at the wide-mouthed expressions of his two oldest children. Laughter would not wait long to follow.

"Well, well, what have we here? So this is how you celebrate the First Day of the Holidays: by launching a surprise attack on your old Dad!"

They soon learned the whole story: the shopper they had pummeled a few moments before was Dad himself. He had reacted quickly, seeing the coming disaster, and, as much to his own surprise as to theirs, had managed to catch their coats before the crash.

They began helping Dad recover his fallen packages. A little boy in an Eton suit had witnessed the spectacular crash, and now had to be dragged away from the scene, finding it all more interesting than getting his Christmas pictures taken. He waved goodbye as he was taken away, and Joshua waved back in sympathy.

"What are you doing here, Dad?" asked Rachel.

"A bit of lunch-hour Christmas shopping," said Dad. "But let's step back into the store, to keep you two from getting soaked, and we'll talk for a minute."

Inside, they realized that they were in the *Bethlehem Toys and Treasures,* the undisputed champion of toy stores, according to all the Kirk kids. Much smaller than the Wiseman's store, it made up for its size with number and variety: every bit of floor, wall, and ceiling space was filled with toys of every kind, but so cleverly arranged that there was still plenty of room for walking, looking, trying, and buying.

On a nearby shelf, packed to bursting (yet with perfect neatness) with board games, Joshua saw what he wanted most of all for Christmas: a brand new game just introduced that year: *Risk.* He had played it at a friend's house a few weeks before, and enjoyed it so much that it had taken the top spot on his Christmas list. It was a game of strategy and creative thinking, which was just what Joshua liked: much better than most of the mindless games on the shelf.

Rachel glanced around at the shop, seeing if anything caught her eye. On a special display at the end of a row, she saw the toy most desired by all her friends: the brand new "grown up" doll called *Barbie*. Like *Risk,* the Barbie doll was new to toy shops that year, but somehow Rachel had not felt the same strong attraction to *Barbie*. Instead, she found her wish list mostly lined with book titles. At the top of that list was C. S. Lewis' *The Chronicles of Narnia,* especially *The Lion, the Witch and the Wardrobe*. Her family had discovered these books about a year before, checking them out of the library to read at home. But Rachel had loved them so much she wanted to start her own collection. *Bethlehem Toys and Treasures* was the only toy store in town to sell books, and as Rachel glanced toward the wall of bookshelves nearby, she caught a glimpse of *The Lion, the Witch and the Wardrobe* on the third shelf from the top. But a shadow of gloom suddenly wrapped her heart as she remembered the gifts: the gifts given to the children in the book; gifts given by Father Christmas. She turned her eyes from the bookcases, and tried to think about the thousand toys lining the shelves.

But as they let their imaginations run over favorite toys, games, and books, both Rachel and Joshua were suddenly struck by the feeling that they would never get them. Would Santa bring anything this year? *Could* he? Had he ever? Of course, they knew their parents always bought them presents as well, but somehow the very idea of presents seemed different, since their run-in with Lou.

Dad was still laughing at the unexpected collision with his children, and so Rachel and Joshua laughed, too. "So what are you two doing, racing along the streets like that?"

The children briefly related their adventures and announced their Quest. "So now Father Lewis has us after this mysterious book," concluded Joshua, "and that's where we're heading. Have you ever been to the Old Page Bookshop, Dad?"

"Sure, I've been there. It's been too long since I've paid old Ezra a visit, though. Maybe the three of us can go sometime. As for this question of Santa Claus, I have some things to say on the matter, but they'll have to keep for now. I'm due back at work in ten minutes, and this store here is not the right place. We'll talk tonight. In the meantime, if Father Lewis wants you to read this book, I expect you'd better do so." He smiled, and they walked back out into the rain, which was already slacking off a bit.

Dad glanced upwards into the rain, letting it splash on his face. He'd always loved weather, and this love had been easily passed on to his children. "Chesterton once said he liked all kinds of weather, except that kind of weather called 'A Glorious Day,'" Dad said. "I've always felt the same. Storms and thunderclouds and blizzards make me feel alive, somehow. I hear this drizzle might turn into snow later today."

"I hope so!" said Joshua.

Rachel smiled at her father. "I remember, when I was little, I asked you why rain falls out of the sky. I never forgot your answer: *because it's a magic sky,* you said."

"And so it is," said Dad, beaming down at her. He was always slightly surprised when his children remembered something he'd told them, though it happened often enough. "Did you ever stop to think how strange it is that water, the very thing we need to live, falls right out of the sky? If you told that story on some rainless planet, they'd laugh at you for believing in fairy tales."

"What would you say to that?" said Rachel, though she knew the answer.

"I'd tell them they're right: I *do* believe in Faerie Tales."

"And in magic?" said Joshua, holding his breath.

"Of course," said Dad. "Be certain of this: the death of magic is the birth of unbelief. To see the wonder *in* the world, we must learn to see the wonder *behind* the world."

Rachel thought of at least three questions she wanted to ask in response to this, but there was no time. "Dad," she said, "we *have* to talk about Santa Claus tonight, okay? I mean, let's not get busy and forget or anything."

Dad took her mittened hand and patted it; then, on a second impulse, kissed it. "We certainly will," he said. "I can see this is important to you, and I won't neglect it. In fact, it's something that's been in the back of my mind to talk about for quite some time, now. Should've taken care of it before, and maybe you'd have been better prepared to deal with little Lou."

"That's okay. Thanks, Dad."

The children waved goodbye, and started off down the street, more slowly this time, heading eastward to their destination. "Don't forget to be home by 5:00, so we can go get our Christmas tree before dinner!" Dad called after them. They we-willed over their shoulders and continued on. Dad followed them with his eyes; then, quite suddenly, his smile vanished. He stood for a while, watching his children, his thoughts fixed on them, and on others.

Chapter Seven

Ghosts

"Joshua," said Rachel as they continued east on Stable Road, "Do you really think this bookshop is haunted?"

Joshua glanced at her. "Why? You're not scared, are you?" His words were not crafted for mockery or teasing; rather, he asked the question because he was curious, and wanted to see if her answer helped explain the tingle of gooseflesh that had been crawling all over him since they left the Library. It was not fear, he thought, but...well, he wasn't quite sure what it was.

"Well," answered Rachel, then paused. After a few moments, she said, "Well, yes, if you want to know. I am scared. Aren't you?"

Joshua wanted to be honest. "No, not really," he said. "Or not much. I'm more...I don't know...excited, I think. I've *always* wanted to see a ghost, or an angel, or a UFO, or something like that. I think it would be neat."

Rachel stared at him a moment as they walked. "Really? I never knew that. That kind of surprises me." She didn't add that this was because her brother tended to be afraid of things that didn't bother her at all: snakes, heights, and the like.

Joshua shrugged. "It never came up, I guess. But I'm surprised too, that you're afraid of ghosts."

"Why?"

"Well, I just...I thought...I always thought you weren't scared of anything."

Rachel smiled despite her nervousness. "That's not true," she said. "I'm scared of plenty of things. Especially...you know, ghosts and stuff. Even angels."

"Angels? Why?"

"I don't know. It's hard to explain. But you know how, in the Bible, when people meet angels, they're always afraid? And the angels usually have to say "fear not," to keep them from being too frightened."

"Yeah," said Joshua. "I always thought that was weird."

"Not me," said Rachel, her voice trembling a bit. "I understand how they felt."

Father Lewis had told the children to continue on Stable Road until they came to the very last little turn to the right. They found it easily enough: it was really no more than an alley, barely wide enough for the two of them to walk abreast. Shadows seemed to surround it. To the right of the alley was a blank brick building, with no door or window to be seen. To the left was a long, tall, wooden structure, the last building of the town, apparently a large storage shed of some kind.

Peering into the tiny lane, they could see only darkness and shadows, vague shapes of trash cans and discarded wooden pallets. Dust hung in the air at the edge of the alley. A teasing sort of fear drifted out of it like invisible smoke. They looked around them. Shoppers lined the busy Christmas streets of Bethlehem, and the sights and smells and noises of conversation and music and general holiday cheer were still within reach; but no one seemed to notice the two children poised at the entrance to the passage.

Rachel felt in her bones—or was tempted to feel—that some nameless horror waited within. Her thoughts drifted back to the conversation at the Library: *even Father Lewis believes this place is haunted.* But what else had he said? "There is no reason for you to be afraid."

Still, she *felt* afraid. Even Joshua felt a surge of fear as they gazed into the alley, though not nearly as strong as Rachel's. Rachel, brave as a lion when it came to any mere physical dangers, trembled at the thought of entering the alley. For her, walking into that dark corridor felt like leaning over the balcony at the top of a twenty-story building would have felt to someone afraid of heights. Joshua, on the other hand, a bit more cautious about things his sister didn't mind, actually enjoyed the mild tingle of terror, which worked on him more like a fascination, an overpowering desire to see the unseen.

Joshua hesitated, knowing that this moment was harder for his sister than for him. He glanced at her face, and was glad to see strength and resolve in her eyes. Even gladder still that she turned her face to the darkness and was the first to step inside. Joshua followed her.

They had never felt anything like this. No one was to be seen; no one anywhere; yet the feeling of being watched—watched and closely studied—was overwhelming. They could almost hear the whispers back and forth:

Who are they?

Why are they here?

How dare they come here?

What shall we do to them?

Not that they actually heard these words with their ears, nor that each one heard, or imagined they heard, the same words as the other. But both felt that such words, or something like them, were being whispered, or at least *thought,* by someone nearby.

"No," whispered Rachel aloud. "It's just our imagination."

Joshua wanted to say, "What if it's not?" But he kept this to himself, not wanting to make things worse for her.

Instead, he whispered back, "Don't be afraid. Whoever they are, they won't...hurt us. They can't." The children grasped each other's hands, and walked on. The alley was so narrow that Rachel's left shoulder was scraping the wooden sides of the storage building, and Joshua's right shoulder was brushing against brick. A shadow flickered in the corner ahead, and their eyes darted after it; too late. Nothing there. The whispered voices—if voices they were— seemed to be further away now, but still chattering on horribly. The children thought perhaps they were moving on, away from them. It was probably just a noise from some unseen window, somewhere.

Who are you?

The voice was right on their necks, like a breath of icy wind. They jumped, hearts racing and skin crawling. Rachel held back a bursting scream, but could not keep in a violent gasp. They turned at the sound, their faces toward the dimly-lit entrance to the alley. As he turned, Joshua thought he saw a face near the entrance, a face with a wide grin like a jack o' lantern's; but his eyes were unfocused and doubtful in the dark, and after a moment, as Joshua's eyes cleared, the face vanished.

"Did you see that?" Rachel said. Her hand clung tightly to her brother's.

"Yes," said Joshua.

"What was it?"

"I don't know. Probably just a kid walking by the alley."

"But what about the voice?"

Even Joshua was trembling a bit at this point. "I'm not sure, Rachel. But I think...well, it could be anything. Maybe we're hearing voices through an air duct or something. Let's go on," he added. "It's all right. There's nothing to be afraid of."

About forty feet from the entrance, barely visible in the darkness, they found a high wooden gate. They looked up to the top, and now saw why the alley was so shrouded in shade: the entire top of the passage was covered by thick tree branches that had grown right over the tops of the two buildings. The wooden gate had been built to cover the entire height of the wall, its top disappearing in the black branches above them. Though tall, the gate was narrow, matching the width of the alley. A brass doorknob stood out from the exact middle of the door. Joshua shined his small flashlight on it: it was in the shape of a crowned head, a bearded king that reminded them of pictures of Alfred or Charlemagne. The children liked it, and it gave them a small flicker of comfort in that dark place. Joshua grasped the doorknob, and it was like seizing a block of ice. He quickly turned it, and opened the gate.

Light burned their eyes through the opening, leaving them just as blind as they had been in the darkness. But the fear of the alley behind hurried them on, and they walked through the gateway, Joshua shutting the door behind them.

Now they could see at last, and were astonished by what they saw. They were now in a clean, well-kept lane. A flower bed filled with a variety of winter blossoms, including the snowdrops so beloved of the children's mother, graced the right wall, and there was even a small transplanted tree. The wall was painted a beautiful shade of dark green. On their left, the wooden storage building had ended, and only a waist-high wooden fence carried on the alley boundary on that side. Over this they could see the fields and forests outside town. The Bethlehem River sparkled in the middle distance, and mountains loomed behind it. They were at the very eastern edge of town. Winter Wrens sang boisterously in unseen trees. There were no shadows or whispers here. On their right, the brick wall extended another twenty feet or so beyond the gate, and there, at the very end of the alley, they found a locked door. It looked to be made of some strong, dark wood; mahogany, perhaps. At the top of the door, barely visible to them even in the sunlight, there were three small, carved letters: TOP. They might easily have missed them.

"Is that somebody's weird sense of humor, or is it telling us we're in the right place?" asked Rachel with a bit of a grin.

"Both, I think," said Joshua. He tried to open the door, but it was locked, and the knob was so tightly anchored to the door that it barely moved.

For several minutes, they tried opening it on their own. For some reason it took a little time for them to think of the obvious thing to do, but in that strange place it was not so obvious. In the end, though, they did think of it: they knocked on the door.

Instantly, the door swung gently open, with barely a sound. They prepared themselves to speak to whoever had opened it, but no one was there. It seemed the door had been mechanically rigged in such a way that it would swing open when anyone simply knocked.

Now they stepped in through the doorway. After the bright sunlight outside, the world inside the door seemed very dark; but as their eyes adjusted, they saw that there were curious shafts of light here and there, evidently from lamps just out of sight. Once they got used to it, they found that they could see well enough, and that the overall effect was cheerful and comforting. Light and darkness alike seemed carefully and even artistically positioned here, as on a skillfully painted canvas: the light was a light of silent contemplation, not of bright parties; the darkness was a darkness of peaceful solitude, not of secret evil. They were in a room about the size of a small chapel, and the smell of the place was like old wood, rich and lovely. And then they saw the books: thousands and thousands of them, on tables, and on shelves. And in bookcases: some small, some reaching to the ceiling. They were in the Old Page Bookshop at last.

Chapter Eight
The Old Page

Rachel and Joshua stood still for a few minutes. There was no one around that they could see. But there was something else: a prickly sense of presence that their eyes and ears and noses could not account for. Someone was nearby, of that they were certain. Both felt at the same moment the urge to simply listen. And after a short time of intense listening, they began to hear something:

Whispered words, and pages turning,

Ghostly sighs and mutterings...

...as the old poem has it. They could distinctly hear someone whispering and turning the pages of a book. But there was no one in the room: all the tables and chairs were visible, and there were no free-standing shelves or furniture behind which the whisperer might be hiding.

"Do you hear that?" said Rachel. "Someone whispering?"

"Yes, I hear it," said Joshua. They were both whispering themselves.

Hand in hand, they took a few steps further in. Again, the presence of someone nearby was very strong: there was a feeling of watchfulness in the Old Page that nearly took their breath away. The whispering and page-turning went on, but still the children could see no one who could be making the noises. There was one silver-colored door on the opposite wall that led out, presumably to other parts of the shop. But it was closed fast, and there was no one else in sight. On their right was a large, ornate, wooden counter, with more stacks of books and a ladder and chair behind it. They peeked over this, but there was no one there, either. They were alone, except for God, and whoever was muttering over a book.

They knew there were a number of different possibilities: maybe the voice was drifting in from another room through a vent in the wall; maybe the owner was rather eccentric and had made a record of himself whispering, and then played it to add a mysterious mood to the store. Maybe there was someone nearby that they just couldn't see for some reason. But none of these explanations were convincing, as far as the children were concerned. They had no doubt that they were in the presence of ghosts, and the knowledge sent shivers coursing through their bodies.

But they were not shivers of fear, or not exactly fear. "Dread" was the word Rachel used long after to describe it, but she was quick to add that it was not a dread of terror. Different than the feeling she'd had in the alley, it was more the feeling one might have in the presence of an angel. For the first time in her life, Rachel understood the difference. She had always thought she would be equally scared upon seeing either an angel or a ghost—perhaps the ghost would be more ugly or horrible, but that didn't bother her much. It was simply the thought of being in the presence of something beyond this world that terrified her. Yet now she sensed the difference: whether it was an angel or a ghost that now confronted them, she did not know; but she realized quickly enough that there was no evil in this place, unless it was brought in from the outside.

Joshua, too, found something unexpected in the shop. He had always thought that seeing a ghost, or an angel, would be the most exciting thing that could happen, and he had secretly thought Rachel's fear a bit silly; he now saw that the whole thing might be scarier than he had thought. But in this place, he found both feelings pulling at him, stretching, but not tearing, his heart.

Whatever spirits might be about the shop, neither Rachel nor Joshua believed they were in an evil place at all; but the fear—or dread, or whatever—was something that could be unpleasant, if they let it. And to both children, it seemed that they were offered a moment of choice, as if they were being asked to choose whether they liked The Old Page Book Shop, and all the strange feelings that came with it—or not. They very quickly decided that they liked it very much indeed.

Slowly, like a dream, the whispering faded. For several minutes there was complete silence. The children glanced around at the books on the shelves and tables, but their minds were still on the ghostly voice. Then the door on the opposite wall opened and through it walked a man who looked as if he had just stepped out of a Dickens book. The top of his head was hairless, but long, white hair flowed down from the back and sides, matched by white mutton chop whiskers. He was wearing small, round eyeglasses, and a very old-fashioned jacket and waistcoat over a white shirt. He was carrying a small stack of books; and when he saw the children, he smiled, but there was also a look of surprise on his face.

"Good afternoon, children, and Merry Christmas to ye." They were somehow not surprised to hear an English accent in his speech.

"Merry Christmas," said the children.

"Welcome to The Old Page Bookshop" he said, as he set the books on the counter. "And welcome indeed! It is not often I see children in this place—not because they're not as welcome as Christmas itself, you understand, but because a lot of the young folk in town seem to believe that my shop is haunted."

Rachel and Joshua glanced at each other. "We've heard that too," said Joshua. "Are you Mr. Tome, then?"

"I am," he said, with a courtly bow, "Ezra Tome, proprietor, at your service. So, you have heard The Old Page was haunted, and yet you came anyway. Why, if I may ask? Do you not believe in ghosts?"

"Well..." said Rachel, thinking carefully. "We were taught not to be afraid of them. And the man who sent us here told us there was nothing to fear."

"Ah, indeed!" said Mr. Tome. "And who might this wise gentleman be?"

"Father Lewis of Saint Augustine Church," said Joshua.

"Oh, Father Lewis! Well, now I understand."

"Mr. Tome," said Rachel, "are the stories true? Is your book shop haunted?"

"Oh, yes, it certainly is haunted. I have heard things here, and felt things. And I have even seen things. What's more, I have heard, felt, and seen things in the presence of others, even very skeptical others: folks who don't believe in ghosts at all. But even they could not deny what they saw."

"And what was that?" said Joshua, though he believed he already knew the answer.

"They saw something that I have seen at other times: a human form: a man, dressed in very old-fashioned clothes—though who is Ezra Tome to talk about old-fashioned, you may think!—old-fashioned clothes, I say, like they wore in the Middle Ages, sitting at a table, poring over books, turning pages, and whispering to himself."

"We heard him!" said Joshua excitedly. "When we first came in here."

"Yes, I don't doubt that you did. The old fellow is heard more often than he is seen. Indeed, I only see or hear him near Christmas."

"And you've seen him?" asked Rachel.

"Oh, yes. It's always the same: 'long about Christmas time, I'll begin to hear the whispering and page-turning. And once in a while—maybe twice each year, or maybe thrice; sometimes only once or not at all—but once in a while, I'll look up, and there, across the room, he'll be sitting, muttering over his books as if he's pondering over deep matters from ancient times."

"But who is he?"

"Well, I don't rightly know, as he's never introduced himself. To tell you the truth, he never quite seems to notice me. If I move, or blink, well, then, he's not there anymore, is he? I never see him for more than a moment or two."

"And how long has he, um, lived, in your shop?" asked Rachel.

"Oh, off and on for the past six or seven years, I think."

"Is he the only ghost you have, then?"

"Well, I don't know," said Mr. Tome, scratching his whiskers, "though I think not. Anyway, he's the most visible. I've run this shop nigh on forty years, now, and I've heard voices and seen shadows from the beginning. But he's the only one I've ever really *seen:* I mean seen so clearly that I could make out his clothes, and the shape of his face, and all that."

"So you don't know his name, I suppose?" said Joshua.

"Not for certain. Though Old Cass always calls him William of Leyland. But he won't ever tell me why." The shopkeeper chuckled to himself.

Joshua and Rachel looked at each other quickly, both trying to recall why those names sounded so familiar. It was Rachel who first remembered: "Those are the names Ms. Track mentioned!" she whispered. Then in a louder voice she addressed Mr. Tome. "Who is Old Cass, Mr. Tome?"

"Old Cass is...well, I suppose you could say he's my best customer." He chuckled as if he'd just made a joke. "Up here every day I'm open."

Rachel smiled. "Buys a lot of books, eh?"

Mr. Tome smiled back. "Not one."

Rachel found this enigmatic, but decided to let it pass. "Can you tell us what happened when your skeptical visitors saw the ghost? You see, we have a friend...or, well, a classmate, anyway, who is always making fun of kids who believe in anything supernatural."

"Well, it was the Anti-Superstition League, wasn't it?" said Mr. Tome. "A couple of the leaders of that bunch—a gentleman and a lady, it was—came by one day, oh, couple of years ago, I believe, and started asking me about my shop, and when it was built, and wasn't it haunted, and all that. And I told them just what I told you. And then they said, 'Mr. Tome, we're here to help you.' And I said that was mighty kind of them, but that I didn't need any help that I could think of, though if they wanted to come back in the Spring, I could put them to a bit of roofing work. But that wasn't what they had in mind, seemingly. 'We're here to prove to you that there are no such things as ghosts, and so you don't have to live in fear anymore.' Well, I laughed at that, and told them they had got their stories mixed up, for I wasn't afraid of any ghosts. That seemed to confuse them, and they huddled together for a while and whispered to each other, as if they weren't sure what to do. Then they said, 'Well, if you're not afraid, you're just deluded, and either way, we want to help. Can we come back tonight and observe what happens in your shop? I think we can prove to you that there is a perfectly natural explanation for whatever you're seeing or hearing.'

"Well, I told them there was no need to wait until the night; that the ghosts were just as likely to be seen and heard in the daytime. But I think they'd seen too many horror films or something, and they had their hearts set on coming back after dark. So I told them that would be fine, that I would be here. And they came back shortly after sundown, and sat and listened and watched. And when they started hearing things, they began to tap on the walls and listen at doors with some special earmuffs they had, and peer into corners through some scientific-type spectacles, and I don't know what else. But this didn't seem to help them much. After a couple of hours, *he* came. William of Leyland, if that's his name (I'm not inclined to doubt Old Cass's word). They heard him first, of course, and scampered all over the room trying to figure out where the voice was coming from. I saw them getting all flustered and sweaty, and the gentleman actually accused me of hiding a record player and speakers somewhere in the room, if you'll believe me. But the lady said their scientific instruments ought to have found the wires, if that was the case. Then, William of Leyland showed up. They saw him, at the end of the hall, and still he whispered and turned those pages. And that really scared them. But to their credit, they both crept nearer, nearer, until they were only a few feet away from him. Then—and this surprised me as much as them for it's never happened, before or since—William looked up and smiled at them. Then he vanished clean away. There was nothing left in the room but the books. At that the lady screamed and ran out of the shop, and the gentleman fainted dead away." He laughed at the thought, and fell silent.

"That's a remarkable story," said Rachel. "Whatever happened to those two people?"

"The funny thing is," said Mr. Tome, "the gentleman woke up a few minutes later and couldn't remember a thing. Or at least he *said* he couldn't. I heard later he told his friends that he had struck his head on a bookcase in the dark, and was knocked unconscious, but that he never found any evidence of ghosts in the shop. As for the lady who ran out screaming, well, she's still around, ringing a Salvation Army bell outside Herod's General Store on Stable Road."

Joshua and Rachel blinked in unison and then gave each other a wide-eyed look. "Ms. Track!" said Rachel. "So...that's why she quit the Anti-Superstition League and gave up teaching. And that's how she knew about William of Leyland—she'd actually seen him! She must have met Old Cass, too."

"Yes, that was her name. Gloria Track, though I hear she has other names among the crueler children in town." Joshua looked uncomfortable at this, and scratched his neck. "And I can't remember the gentleman's first name," continued Mr. Tome, "but his last name was Nyten. I believe he was and is the president of the Anti-Superstition League."

"Lou's Dad!" said Joshua, and Rachel nodded.

Mr. Tome peered over his eyeglasses at Joshua and Rachel. "You two are the best-informed children I've ever had in my shop." He chuckled again. "But yes, that was a fine day, when the ASL came by. Fun for me, but also good for *them,* too, if only they could step down from their lecterns for a minute and have a laugh at themselves, as we all must, from time to time. But they seldom do. Gloria Track was something of an exception, though I believe she still has some way to go yet in her recovery."

"What do you mean?" asked Rachel.

"Well, it seems to me that Ms. Track has only traded one sort of superstition for another. To put it another way, she's gone from believing in nothing to believing in everything. See, those hobby scientists at the ASL aren't the only ones fighting against superstition, no indeed. I'm just as set against it as they ever were. The problem with the Anti-Superstition League is that they don't really know what superstition is."

Joshua found this an intriguing statement. "Can you explain that, please?"

Mr. Tome leaned against the counter. "Well, you see, to some modern men, superstition means believing in ghosts, or angels, or faeries, or gods. They themselves refuse to believe in anything they can't find with their senses, or argue into existence out of their brains. By their reckoning, nearly every human being in history, including the great men who built the Western World, were backwards, superstitious fools."

With his next words, the shopkeeper waved his hands around at the books on the shelves. "Think of it! Augustine, Dante, Copernicus, Calvin, Kepler, Shakespeare, Bach—churls and chawbacons, the lot of them. And now comes the ASL to tell us that *they,* and their make-believe scientists, are here to rescue us from St. Paul and King Alfred, and the rest." He laughed aloud. "That's why that day with the ASL was so very agreeable."

"But Mr. Tome," said Joshua, "if superstition doesn't mean believing in ghosts, and stuff like that, what *does* it mean?" He was still smarting a bit from having been called superstitious by Lou, son of the ASL's president.

"Well, lad, superstition means believing that magic rules the world, and not God. See, I don't deny that there is magic *in* the world, but I do deny that magic *runs* the world. That's why it's superstitious, and silly, to think you've caused yourself bad luck by spilling salt, or crossing paths with a black cat. But believing that God rules the world through the magic of His own power and providence—that's an entirely different matter, as nearly all the great minds of history would tell ye."

"Mr. Tome," said Rachel, who had just remembered something. "Our Sunday School teacher once told us there can't be any such things as ghosts, since people either go to Heaven or Hell when they die."

"So they do," replied the shopkeeper, "But that doesn't mean they can't come back—if God wants 'em to. Have ye never heard how Samuel, the old judge and prophet, came back to speak to Saul on the eve of his death? Now, of course, it would be wrong to try to *call* the dead, to bring them back, like the Witch of Endor did with Samuel. But if *God* sends them, well, that's quite different, now, isn't it?'

"But why would He?"

"Who knows? But we know that He did send Moses and Elijah back once, don't we? And consider this: part of the misery of Hell might be the remorseful reliving of evil deeds done on earth. In this way, the poor ghosts might be here, even where we can see them; and yet they never leave Hell, nor do the living cross the gulf to go there. Of course, I don't know how it works any more than you do. I'm content to leave all that up to the Good Lord."

He smiled and took a step or two away from the counter, and leaned down with his hands on his knees, so that his face was about on a level with the children.

"But here am I, chattering on, when I haven't even found out why you're here! Father Lewis sent you, you say. What is it you're looking for?"

Chapter Nine

The Book

Joshua took a step forward and spoke. "Father Lewis told us to ask for something called *The Nicholas Book*," he said.

"I see," replied the shopkeeper. "I might have guessed. You have questions about Father Christmas, eh?"

"Yes sir."

He smiled. "Come with me, then. I'll show you where it is."

They obeyed, and walked behind Ezra Tome as he led them through the silver door. Here they could see that the room they had been in was only a sort of a parlor; but now they were in the heart of the book shop. And it was bigger than they had imagined. Yet somehow, at any given spot, they felt that here one could browse among the shelves, or sit in one of the antique chairs, and feel as cozy as if he were in his own den or library at home.

"There's hardly anyone here this afternoon," Mr. Tome said, "though Old Cass comes up here practically every day. Haven't seen him yet today, but he may have slipped in while I was in the back. He knows this place as well as I do."

Mr. Tome led them through row after row of books, and through so many rooms they lost count. As the shopkeeper had indicated, the place was almost empty, though here and there bright eyes and ready smiles flashed at them from a table or behind a bookcase. There was no doubt to either of the children that this place was friendly to them, and, even more so, *good*. But that didn't stop them from feeling, as Rachel later put it, that "there was something awful and terrible just around the corner—but I mean that in a good way." They could get no closer to it in words, but the feeling caused them both to speak in whispers, even though there was evidently no requirement to do so, and Mr. Tome himself certainly did not. There was simply a sense of overpowering presence there, as if the shop itself were somehow alive.

Finally they arrived at a door painted blue. On the right side of the door there was a little shelf, with a small wooden box and a little silver bell. Before entering, Mr Tome reached up to the box, opened it, and took out three candles. He lit these, and gave one to each of the children, keeping one himself. "There's no electric lights back here," he said, "or windows. So you'll have to use these." He smiled, and opened the door.

This was not the largest room they had yet seen (though it was large enough), but it seemed taller, the ceiling shadow-shrouded, as if concealing secret rooms in the rafters. Besides the door through which they entered, there were two doorless entryways, one on the left hand wall, and one on the right. Only a dim, shadowy sort of light entered the room from these: and even with the light from the open doorway and the candles in their hands, they could see little of the room. No one seemed to be inside. As they walked into the room they could see that the walls were lined with built-in bookshelves, but most of the room was filled with tall, narrow bookcases that towered over them. In that dim place they reminded Rachel very much of trees, and she had the strange feeling that they were walking in a great forest at night.

Mr. Tome stopped in the left-hand corner of the room near the back door. They knew it was the back door because it was green, with letters painted in gold: *Back Door*. In the corner, only a few feet away from the door, there was a little table and three chairs. Mr. Tome gestured to them to have a seat, and they did so. On the table were three candlesticks, and the children and Mr. Tome set their candles in these. Then, he walked to the opposite corner, on the other side of the backdoor, to a large bookcase just beside another table.

It was filled, as was every other bookcase and shelf in this room, with manuscripts: most of these were leather-bound, but some, much older-looking, were in scroll form. Ezra Tome selected a book bound in dark red leather, and eased it gently off the shelf. Then he set it down on the table before Rachel and Joshua.

It was not very large, or thick; it looked almost like a small diary or journal. It was trimmed in gold, but both the red and gold were faded. It appeared to be old, but not ancient. There was no title or words of any sort on the cover or spine.

"Here it is," said Mr. Tome. "And in case Father Lewis didn't already tell you, I must advise you that it is not for sale. It's to reside here in the shop, but not leave: those were my instructions."

"That's fine," said Rachel, with a smile. "We can read it here. Thank you."

"There are more candles just outside the door, if you need them," said the shopkeeper, "and I believe you saw the little bell? Good. If you need anything, just give it a shake or two. I'll hear it."

He smiled, bowed, and left them, off to other work in others parts of his shop.

When the door shut, the children were left with a great deal of darkness, a little light, and complete silence. Rachel shuddered as a chill swept over her. Never had she been in a place that felt more haunted than this. Joshua felt it too. Yet once again, they could not bring themselves to think of anything evil dwelling in that place.

They took a deep breath, and nodded to each other. Joshua reached out his hand to open the book. But just then something in the corner of his eye stopped him: a flicker of light in the opposite corner, on the wall near the blue door. There was no sound on that carpeted floor, but there was movement. Joshua swallowed hard, and Rachel held her breath. The light was coming toward them.

Chapter Ten

Imagination

Joshua and Rachel were as still as statues, waiting to see what would happen next. After a few seconds, the light emerged from behind a book case, and they saw that it was illuminating the figure of a man: a very small, frail, stooped, old man. As he came closer to them, they could see that he labored along, leaning on a cane with one hand; while the other hand held a candle in a brass stick. The children could not see his face. He appeared to be so thin and weak that they wondered he could walk at all. He stopped, still just in the shadows, and then suddenly leaned forward with the candle stick near his head, so that his face seemed to lunge out of the darkness and into the light at them. The children jumped a little at this strange and sudden movement. But the face was kindly and bore a smile, and the old man chuckled.

"Fear not, children!" he said. "I was only having a bit of fun." Though the man looked to be at least ninety, his teeth gleamed white and straight in the candlelight. He was wearing a gray suit, but a bright blue tie stood out sharply from within his white shirt. He chuckled again, more from habit than humor, it seemed, and drew nearer to them.

"Well, good afternoon," he said.

"Good afternoon, sir," returned the children, rising in courtesy as the elderly man approached.

"I heard old Ezra from back there," he pointed his cane toward the far corner, which could not actually be seen because of the tree-like bookcases in front of it, "Heard him talking about *The Nicholas Book*. Been a long time—more than a year—since anyone's looked at it. Besides me, of course."

"You've read it, then?" asked Rachel.

"Many times," he answered with a smile. "You might say *The Nicholas Book* is my favorite book in the shop." He chuckled again, though there seemed no reason to do so.

"Won't you sit down, sir?" offered Rachel, who felt that they should not miss a chance to talk to someone who knew the book well.

"Oh, for a spell, I suppose," said the old man, easing delicately into the third chair. "Thank you kindly."

"I'm Rachel, and this is my brother, Joshua."

"I'm mighty pleased to know you, Rachel, and Joshua," he said. "Folks around here call me Old Cass. I hope you will, too."

"Oh, yes, Mr. Tome mentioned you."

"Did he, now?"

"Yes, he said hardly anyone was in the shop today, but he expected you were probably here somewhere." She smiled understandingly. "From what he said, I guess this is your favorite place!"

Old Cass chuckled again. "No. No, it's not." His eyes blinked, and refocused: the children could tell those eyes were seeing something else, something far off but very real. Something beautiful: Old Cass's favorite place, whatever it was. "My favorite place is more beautiful than all others, more lovely even than the City of David from star-height." But," he added, "I do enjoy being here as well. It's a fine shop, much better than folks down here usually come up with."

"Are you from up north, then?" said Joshua, picking up on the "down here" phrasing.

"No sir, not at all," said Old Cass, and chuckled again.

"Mr....um, Old Cass," said Rachel. "We came here to read this book. Since you know a lot about it, I wonder if you can help us."

"I would be very pleased to help," he said. "In fact, that is why I came over.

"Thank you. Well, first of all, I was just wondering: why *do* you read the book so much?"

"Hmm, well, I suppose it's my business to read it," he said. "Indirectly, I am the reason this book is here."

He said no more about it, and both children opened their mouths to question further; but something in the old man's face warned them, *not too close. Ask something else.* But both Joshua and Rachel had the same thought: *Old Cass must be the owner of the book, the one Mr. Tome told us about, who wanted him to keep it here, unsold.* And both had the same question: *did Old Cass also write the book?* But they did not ask this question aloud.

"We had some questions about Saint Nicholas," said Joshua. "A friend of ours told us to find this book. He said it would answer some of our questions."

"And certainly it will," said the old man, leaning forward with both hands on his cane. "Though it might also give you some new ones."

"Our friend said that, too. What do you know about Santa Claus?" Joshua continued.

"Much," said Old Cass. "But what in particular do you want to know?"

"Well," said Joshua, "I guess we're trying to find out if Santa Claus is real."

"Well of course he is," said Old Cass. "But then perhaps you've never heard of the Communion of the Saints?"

"Oh, we have," said Joshua, and he related what Father Lewis had said to them.

"Saint Nicholas belongs to that Communion," said Old Cass, nodding his head. "But Santa Claus also belongs to another world as well: the world of Faerie."

Joshua pondered this for a few moments, and Old Cass went silent, watching him, sensing the storm of thought in the young man's mind, and willing to wait for him. Joshua half-remembered something his Mother had said to him once, something like what old Cass had said about Faerie. But he couldn't quite remember, and now he felt puzzled. He looked up at the old man and spoke.

"But what does that mean? Is Santa Claus *just* a fairy tale? If so, then why do you and Father Lewis and everybody keep saying he's real?"

"*Just* a Faerie Tale, young man?" That was all he said: his eyes chased Joshua's, found them, and held them. He waited.

"Well..." Joshua hesitated before saying more. He focused his energies on his mother's words, and some of them began to return to him. "Okay. I didn't mean it like that. My Mom once said that...that..." There it was. "'Good Faerie tales are always true.' I didn't understand what she meant, really. She tried to explain, but...anyway, I think she meant that Faerie Tales always teach us something that *is* true."

"And," added Rachel, "I think she also meant that some stories that are called Faerie Tales *have* come true. Like the story of Jesus."

"Ah, now we approach the truth," said Old Cass, smiling broadly. "And we must also remember that there are some things that *only* Faerie can teach us."

"What do you mean?" asked Joshua.

"I mean," he said, "that there are things we cannot know by scientific observation, or intellectual research. There are different kinds of knowledge, each important in its way. If we want knowledge about a distant star, we look in a telescope. If we want to know about some tiny substance, we look in a microscope. But what telescope or microscope can explain love, or art? And there are things that even a good book of history, or a fine novel, or a philosophical treatise, cannot tell us. Only in the world of Faerie can we know them."

Rachel leaned closer over the table. "What sorts of things?"

Old Cass spoke in a voice only a little louder than a whisper. "The things one learns in that perilous country cannot easily be set down in words and sentences. It is more of an effect on the soul, on the *way* a man thinks and feels and lives and chooses and believes. Long acquaintance with Faerie makes for a different *sort* of man—or child. There are some things—things of Beauty and Wisdom and Faith—that he can only know whose imagination has been baptized."

"Imagination?" said Joshua. "You mean, like pretending?"

"No, no," said Old Cass, shaking his head. "Imagination, young man! The life of the mind and heart, the capacity to dream and create and invent, yes, and reason, too. The God-given power to see beyond the narrow limits of the senses. Imagination! The place of all art and music and philosophy and storytelling and mercy and laughter and war and beauty and love. It is the farthest thing from mere pretending that I can think of."

Joshua was startled by the suddenness of the frail little man's passion, but Old Cass's words seemed to light a fire in the boy's heart, and he longed to know and understand more.

"I think I see," he said. "But how does that happen? How does our imagination get baptized?"

"Only in Faerie—yet the borders of that land extend farther than you might think. There are many today who possess great knowledge, yet their imagination withers. In such men knowledge becomes little more than a catalogue of facts, a trunkful of trivia. With a dry imagination, a man is left with a thirsty soul. Ashes and dust. Dryness."

Speech hid for a while, as the children considered his words. Finally, Joshua spoke once more. "If our...imaginations have been baptized, then what can we know about Santa Claus? I mean, if a Faerie Tale can be true, how do we know if the story of Santa Claus is true?"

Old Cass chuckled as he answered. "The same way you know if any old story is true: the voice of history. Saint Nicholas belongs both to history and to Faerie. So do many others, more than you might think."

Joshua persisted, for he still strained to wrap his mind around all that he was hearing. "Yes, but when we read this book, will we *know?*"

Old Cass looked at him closely, as if trying to decide something. Then he smiled, and put a fatherly hand on the boy's shoulder. "You will know more than you do now, sure. But if you do not look at what you know in the light of Faerie, you will almost certainly misunderstand it. And this shall be a sign unto you: you shall see the glory in the place where you least expected it."

He smiled again, chuckled again, and rose from his chair. "Read the book!" He turned to walk away. With a wave over his shoulder, he said, "I'll be nearby, if you need me. Goodbye for the present!" And so he left them, his boots and cane making no noise on the carpeted floor, and they watched him until the light of the candle disappeared into the dark corner.

Chapter Eleven

Nicholas of Myra

Shadows moved in three places in the room where Joshua and Rachel were reading. Three shadows, all hidden, two of which were oblivious of the others, and all of which were moving toward the children. They only existed as shadows at all because of the dim light of the candles on the little table, and the dimmer light from the two passageways.

One Shadow sat quietly, deciding to bide its time. It wanted to hear what was about to be read, its curiosity awakened, almost against its will. But its time would come, and its plan could wait, at least for a while. Another Shadow wanted only the Book. It knew that when the children had finished reading, they would leave the book there on the shelf. Once they were gone, this Shadow knew that it could easily retrieve the Book, slip out the back door, and no one would be the wiser. But if they did *not* put the book down... then it would *make* them give it up. Until then, it would wait, and listen. As for the Third Shadow, it too waited and listened, watching the others intently.

The time had come to read the book. As they silently pondered all they had heard this day, the children looked at each other, and nodded. "Ready?" said Rachel.

"Ready," said her brother. But before he began, Joshua looked around. The manuscript room seemed so cold, and lonely, and empty. And yet, not quite empty. His eyes peered into the darkness beyond the circle of candlelight. Was someone there? He shook his head, thinking it must be his imagination. He opened the red book to read, not knowing that he was being watched and listened to.

On the first page, they read this:

The following narrative was recorded by Jacob Reuel

24 December, 1925

"More than thirty years ago," said Joshua. "Christmas Eve."

"Let's turn the page," said Rachel.

On the pages that followed, they found these words, in a thin, shaky hand. Joshua read them aloud:

My name is Jacob Reuel, and I am either one hundred and three, or one hundred and four years old. There is some dispute about the year, though both my parents seem to agree that I was in fact born. They are sure of the date, too: Christmas Eve. I write these words on my birthday, because birthdays have always reminded me of the solemn fact that I have one less of them than this time last year; also, because I have received confident word from my doctor that this birthday will certainly be my last. I begin writing at Dawn of the twenty-fourth, hoping to finish by Christmas morning, though my illness and weakness make me rather a slow scribe.

I wish to offer my own story, but first, in order of both importance and chronology, I present the translated text of a very old manuscript. My father was an historian, and he gave this to me on his deathbed many years ago. He died before he could tell me where he'd found it, or how it had come to him; all he said was that it had been a Christmas present. Yet I think I know whence it came. If you will turn to the back of the book, you will find the manuscript. It is in Latin, and very fragile. But on the pages that follow, I will copy out my own translation, made several years ago, for those not acquainted with Latin. My only copy of the translation is in poor condition, and I wish to preserve it more permanently here.

Joshua turned to the back and found a leather pocket sewn into the inside cover of the back of the book. But there was no manuscript. Joshua looked at Rachel, puzzled.

"Never mind," said Rachel. "We'll just read the translation." Joshua turned back to the beginning.

Here, then, is my translation, which I have tried to render with the utmost faithfulness to the original. The author does not name himself, and there are but few clues herein as to his identity. He simply writes. These are his words:

Next followed several pages, with the translated text:

Here follows a brief account of the life of Nicholas, bishop of Myra. I will not reveal my own name, as he would be displeased to find that I have set these things in writing. Yet I judge it good that some small record, at least, should survive. I am grateful to count Nicholas as my dearest friend, and I should be grieved to think I had done him a disservice in any way. Therefore, I will not publish this account, but only pass it on to my son, and so hand the story down throughout my generations. May the Holy and Indivisible Trinity be glorified by, or despite, my feeble, and perhaps foolish, efforts.

Nicholas was born in Patara in Lycia in the year of our Lord two hundred and seventy; that is, just over nine hundred years ago.

"What?" Rachel started at these words.

"What is it?" said Joshua.

"What he just said. If Nicholas was born over nine hundred years before, that would mean this man is writing in...let's see... the 1100s."

"Okay..."

"But he claims to be a *friend* of Nicholas."

The words hung in the air for a few moments, before Joshua said, "Oh. Weird. But that means..."

"Exactly. Let's keep reading."

"Okay." On Joshua read.

His father, Theophanes, was a wealthy man, and he and his wife Nonna raised Nicholas in the faith of Christ. From his youngest days, Nicholas was full of faith and devotion, dedicating his life to the service of his Lord. When his mother and father died in a terrible plague that came upon Patara, Nicholas' namesake and uncle, Bishop Nicholas of Patara, took the boy into his home and continued his education, eventually raising him up to the priesthood.

Nicholas inherited all his father's wealth after his death, but he did not lavish this treasure upon himself. Instead, he spent his time in the study of Holy Scripture, and his money to aid the sick and poor. He made a pilgrimage to Alexandria and Jerusalem, where he studied the Scriptures under the fathers of the church there. When he returned, he ministered for several years in his native Patara, but, while still a young man, was appointed as Bishop of the nearby city of Myra. He preached with great zeal among the people, and many became followers of the Way. And so the church in Myra grew strong.

In the fury of persecution under the wicked emperor, Diocletian, the good bishop was cast into prison, where he remained for some years. But after the glorious conversion of the noble emperor Constantine, Nicholas was released and returned to Myra. Then, in the year of our Lord three hundred and twenty-five, Nicholas was summoned, along with many other Christian shepherds, to the great council in Nicaea. There he boldly defended the doctrine of our Lord's divinity against the heretic Arius. And it is widely known that, when Arius became enfrenzied and would not cease his prattling blasphemies, Nicholas, alone of all those present, had the courage to strike the heresiarch on the mouth and thus to silence him.

I will not long dwell on the many noble deeds of Nicholas, for they are well known, and many of the stories of his life are already recorded in the writings of Bishop Reginald of Eichstaedt (the longer version of his work is said by some to have been lost, but I have myself seen copies at Rome and Heidelberg; other copies exist as well). Suffice it to say that throughout the length and breadth of Christendom no man possessed a better name for mercy, sacrifice, and generosity, than Nicholas of Myra. Nicholas used the fortune he inherited from his father, not for his own use or comfort, but for the succour of the needy . He built orphanages, hospitals, churches, and gave away nearly everything he owned. Well-deserved was his good name. Yet it must be said that this reputation was gained against his will. For following the commands of our Lord, Nicholas performed nearly all his acts of mercy in secret, never letting the beneficiaries of his kindness know to whom they were indebted. But one man—whose three *daughters had received mysterious gifts of gold for their dowry, thus saving them from a life of slavery—this man, I say, sought out his benefactor, setting his face to the task of seeing through the mystery, and made a vow that he would never cease looking until he could thank his patron face to face. And so it was that, in the end, this man found that Bishop Nicholas was the one to whom he owed his gratitude. And though this man realized his desire to thank the savior of his children, Nicholas implored him to secrecy, and bade him show mercy and generosity to others, if he wished to thank God for the gifts. And perhaps the man kept that promise, but somehow, whether through his word, or that of his daughters, or of others, the story became published abroad, and the name of Nicholas became a byword of benevolence throughout the households of Christendom. Nicholas was, of all men, the giver of gifts.*

This grieved Nicholas, and such unasked-for fame hindered his ministry; for, just as a king cannot easily walk among his people, being too well-known and sought-after, so Nicholas, like our Lord before him, found that throngs of boon-seekers greeted him everywhere. Yet he continued on, preaching the Gospel, feeding the poor, and defending the helpless.

I must also say a word about the city of Myra. Though this is largely forgotten today, the city was one of strategic importance in the spiritual battles of ancient times. I know not why; and if Nicholas knows, he has not told me. But howsoever it may be, the city of Myra had at one time been a common battleground between the thrones of Satan and his angelic powers, and the holy angels of our God. And though, as the blessed Apostle has told us, we are no longer under the tutelage of angels, yet many of the evil spirit lords persisted with a feigned authority; and under pretense of such, demanded allegiance as gods over lands and cities they no longer ruled. And many in the city of Myra worshiped one such pretender, styling himself Prince of Myra, the mighty angelic power, ruling, or claiming to rule, under the overlordship of Lucifer.

Now, throughout his life, Nicholas was opposed by the Prince of Myra, just as many other Christian shepherds are opposed by the powers that seek to rule their cities. But the Prince of Myra was hindered by Cassiel and the blessed angels, and found little victory during the time of Nicholas' episcopacy. And that wicked spirit was exceeding wroth, and became maddened in his rage. And so the worshipers of the Prince of Myra were at times also driven mad by his possession of them, and they foamed at the mouth, and cursed and wailed, like the demoniacs in the time of our Lord. And they cursed Nicholas and spoke all manner of evil against him falsely; yet not they, but the Prince of Myra speaking through them. And he set some of them to kill Nicholas, but always these plots were hindered, and Nicholas could not be touched; for so had Heaven decreed.

So the years passed, until Nicholas, now an old man, wracked with pain and sickness, lay upon his deathbed. And he submitted himself to God, and made ready for his departure. And so Nicholas closed his eyes, at the very moment, as it seemed to him, of death.

Chapter Twelve

Enoch and Elijah

And it was then the time of Advent, the sixth of December. But while Nicholas yet lived, he was visited by an angel, Cassiel, the very spirit who with his angelic armies had fought against the Prince of Myra for many earthly years. And he said to Nicholas, "Behold, the Lord hath sent me to you, for it seems good to the King of Heaven to set for you another task, ere you enter wholly into the Heavenly Sabbath rest."

And as Nicholas listened, the angel told him that God desired to keep him, so that he should not see death, but, like Enoch, and Elijah, be caught away to Heaven for a time. And then it would be the Lord's pleasure to send him back again, to continue his work, yet in secret, as he had ever sought. Thus the task set before him was to do as he had done all his life, preaching the Gospel, by words and deeds, and in especial, by acts of mercy and generosity. Cassiel told Nicholas that it was the will of God that he should be a giver of grace-gifts to those in need, and most especially to the undeserving, that the grace of God might be the more magnified. And the angel told him that he was to rest throughout the year, and to labor only during the blessed seasons of Advent and Christmas; for gifts of gold and food and clothing, being material in nature, are surer signs of the holy materiality which robed the Son of God in His Incarnation. Thus would Nicholas, by gifts and deeds, preach the Gospel of Bethlehem through ages and generations.

And Nicholas said, taking the words of our Lord's mother as his own, "Be it unto me according to thy word." And Cassiel then gave to him a gift—a ring of gold set with a red stone. This ring was some of the very last of the gold given to the Christ child by the Magi, and it had been entrusted to Cassiel, one of the very angels who had brought word of the birth of Christ to the Shepherds, and who had attended the Holy Family throughout their lives.

After his season of rest, Nicholas was brought back to this world, and was clothed in scarlet. And he objected to this, protesting that he desired no finery of garment that might draw attention to one called to work in secret. Yet Cassiel overruled him, saying that such were the robes of his office – the scarlet of blood, in honor of the shed blood of our Lord, in whose name alone Nicholas was to labor; and that in any case he could make of his scarlet robes whatsoever sort of clothing he might wish. And so it was that Nicholas, in this his latter life, took the guise of a humble craftsman. Through all the earth he wandered, doing the work of God with great joy, gifted with the life of the longaevi, of whom he is the father and chief. And some say that Nicholas at last made his home in the wild, wintry lands of the far North, where no explorer has ever gone, and some say otherwise. I myself know the truth of this matter, but have sworn never to speak of it.

But the hatred of the Prince of Myra dogged him even in his immortality. And just as Nicholas now wandered through the earth as a wood-shaper, giving to those in need, and stirring up the spirit of sacrifice and mercy, so the Prince of Myra, Captain of the hosts of Satan, took on the guise of a peripatetic scholar, possessing the physical body of first one evil man, and then another, through the centuries, and he followed Nicholas wherever he went, to oppose him and undo his work. And he took to himself the name of Old Nick, in mockery of the saint of Myra. And for a time, Nicholas was hindered and defeated; but then was Cassiel sent to succour him, and to fight against Old Nick; and from that time to this have they hounded and battled one another, never ceasing, for Cassiel and his angels were given to minister to Nicholas, and to protect him at need; while the spirits of Old Nick had sworn wicked oaths that they would not rest, but ever seek to terrorize, madden, or destroy Nicholas, if they might.

But he has endured their scorn and mockery, and all their assaults. And thus today he is justly famous throughout all Christendom, and many look to him for guidance on the seas, or the roads, or for the help and comfort of their children. Nicholas is the saviour, under God, of my own life, and of my family.

He has tutored me, an unlearned man, and raised me up to the priesthood, and taught me the theology and art of joy. And in my conscience I cannot fail to honor him and thank him through all my generations. So to this end have I set down these words: that though he be the secret benefactor of a million, million poor men, yet neither I, who have been graced with the knowledge of his goodness, nor my children, to whom I inscribe this book, should fail in gratitude to God, or to his servant Nicholas, giver of grace-gifts.

The Township of Leyland, St. Stephen's Day, 1171

Chapter Thirteen

Jacob's Christmas

Joshua and Rachel looked at each other in wonder. Some parts of the story they'd just read were familiar; but much of it was new to them, and their eyes revealed the question that both were thinking: *is it true?*

"Rachel, look," said Joshua. "The writer doesn't give his name, but he does say where he's from, or at least where he's writing from: *Leyland.*"

"I noticed that too, said Rachel. "So, what does that mean? That the Medieval manuscript was written by William of Leyland, who now haunts this bookshop?"

"I don't know," said Joshua. "But it sure seems like it."

"Look," said Rachel. "There's more, on the next page. It's Jacob Reuel, the hundred and three—or four—year-old man. Keep reading."

"Okay," said Joshua, and he did.

So ends the tale of our anonymous chronicler. But now I wish to tell you my story, and to tell you how, though I only read the preceding manuscript after I had become an old man, I already knew its story—all of it.

When I was about nine—or ten: I believe I have mentioned before the discrepancy about the year of my birth; about the year 1831, anyway—my father came home one evening a few days before Christmas all a-bother, telling us all to clean up, sit up, and otherwise be on our best behavior, for we were to have a Visitor of some importance in an hour's time. That's all he would say, except that the Visitor was very famous and was an important person in the Church somewhere overseas. But Father looked so excited and mysterious as he spoke that I determined to watch closely and learn all I could about this distinguished guest.

My mother set the table with special splendor that night, and soon enough our Visitor arrived. He was tall and fair, and looked strong and stout, though not at all fat; and I guessed he must have been around sixty, perhaps seventy years old, though at times his eyes made him look younger, and his words made him sound even older. He was dressed in a white tunic, and dark red trousers and jacket that looked rather old-fashioned. His white hair was longer than that worn by men of those days, and he sported a long white beard that reached nearly to his belt. When first he entered he was also clad in a long cloak and hood of the same color as his jacket and trousers. And he wore immense black boots. He spoke perfect English but with a foreign accent that I have never been able to place. Father introduced him simply as Mr. Nicholas of Myra. My Mother recognized the name of the town as the home of the legendary Saint Nicholas and she commented on this coincidence. Mr. Nicholas laughed and said yes, it was the same town.

It didn't take too long for me to decide that Mr. Nicholas was without rival the most delightful and wonderful man I had ever met. As the evening wore on he told stories, cracked jokes, and sang songs (accompanying himself on a lute he had brought with him, an ancient instrument I had never seen before); he even taught us all a simple, yet beautiful country dance that we continued to use as a family for many years thereafter. And he gave us gifts: hand-carved wooden wonders that set the heart racing with their beauty and graceful utility. For my mother, there was a lovely box for organizing thread, needles and other sewing accessories (sewing was Mother's passion), with so many inner boxes and compartments that she was still discovering new ones for years afterwards. For Father, Mr Nicholas had brought a hunting knife with the most exquisitely-carved handle I had ever seen. Father told me many years later that he had never once had to sharpen that knife. And for my brothers and sisters and I there were magnificent toys: dolls and carved horses and ships and dragons and swords, all of the best craftsmanship and *so delightful to the eye that they were almost as pleasant to look at as to play with.*

You may readily guess that my opinion of our wonderful Visitor had rather settled itself before the evening was over. I was convinced in my heart and mind that, however it may be, my Father had become acquainted with the legendary, but real—I was quite sure of that now—Saint Nicholas himself: Father Christmas as he is known to some, Santa Claus to others.

My heart raced with magic and excitement at the thought. Santa Claus himself was in my house! But why, then, had Father not told us? Did he imagine we could not judge the truth for ourselves? Or perhaps he felt it only polite to allow Mr. Nicholas to say as much or little about himself as he would? Perhaps. But this was a bit much to ask of a nine (or ten) year old boy who has just made such a remarkable discovery. So as Father and Mother and Mr. Nicholas talked over coffee after dinner, and we children had been sent to bed, I, as the eldest, took it upon myself to creep back downstairs. This took some courage, for Mother was adamant about bedtimes, but I spoke respectfully and forthrightly, and my parents allowed me to approach. I had a question, I told them, for Mr. Nicholas. With our Visitor's kind permission, Father allowed me to speak.

"Mr. Nicholas," I said, my heart thumping heavily and my voice trembling, "are you...are you Santa Claus? I mean, are you really Saint Nicholas, the one who brings Christmas presents to our house every year?"

Father started to protest that such a question was not appropriate, but Mr. Nicholas held up a hand, and said he didn't mind answering. "I will tell you what I can, my young friend," he said, "for in some matters I am bound, by promise, to silence. My name is Nicholas, and I serve the Lord Jesus Christ as a minister of His grace. I lived for some years in the city of Myra, a Greek city that is now part of the Ottoman Empire. I still regard Myra as my hometown, though my work takes me all over the world.

"I am also a wood-worker, for I love the trees of our Creator, most beautiful of all His handiwork, in my eyes. Their beauty is extended and reborn when I harvest the wood of those trees and

make such things as I hope will bring service and joy to those who use them: tools and toys, so to speak. I can also tell you that I am old, far older than I appear, and far older than your men of medicine would think possible. Our Lord has shown much grace to me, an unworthy servant."

At this, he stopped speaking, but of course, his words were as much as a confession to my youthful mind, and I was convinced of who he was. Yet a dozen questions more I could have asked, but I could only splutter out a few of them. "But Mr. Nicholas," I said, "do you bring toys to our house on Christmas Eve? How did you meet Dad? And do you often visit people before Christmas?"

As an answer, he began to tell me the history of his life, and it was here that I first heard all of what you have read in the twelfth-century manuscript that my father gave me much later. As he spoke of Cassiel's visit, I noticed for the first time the flash of gold on his finger, and the red fire of the stone. My heart drummed faster at the thought: the Magi's gold!

As he finished his tale, I sat silent, dumb with amazement at what I had just heard. And I considered that there were yet greater wonders still: wonders Mr Nicholas had left out of his tale because of his promise to remain silent! I looked at my father, and he shook his head and smiled at me, obviously just as astonished as I was at the remarkable Providence that had brought a legend to life in our very own parlour.

Only one more question remained, and I asked it: "Mr. Nicholas, why are you telling us all this? I mean, sir, why us?" You will understand that I was grateful to be privy to this great tale, but in light of all I had just heard, it seemed strange that Mr. Nicholas, so secretive in his work, should show up in our house to tell the full tale.

"I tell you this story because I must," was his reply. "If I could work my own will in this matter, I should always move about in silence, invisible to mortal life. But about thirty years ago, Cassiel the messenger returned to me on the first Sunday of Advent. He told me that my enemy, Old Nick, was laying plans for a new attack: this time he would seek to destroy my work through lies. And in order to fight those lies, Cassiel laid upon me this requirement: that *each year, I should find a few willing families to listen to the true story of my life and work. These families may choose to believe or not believe the tale I tell them; but in this way, Cassiel hopes to counter, in some small measure, the deceptions of Old Nick."*

But what lies was Old Nick telling? I wondered. Mr. Nicholas answered that question as well. And it was in this way that I learned much that the twelfth-century chronicler of Leyland could never have known. But I feel my heart and hands growing weaker, and I know that time is short. Briefly, then: after countless battles with Cassiel over the fate of Nicholas, Old Nick's next idea was simply to expose Nicholas: he made his name widely known; made him famous, in fact, so that Nicholas' desire to work in secret was remarkably thwarted, as it had once been in the days of his earlier life. Because of this, Nicholas had spent many years in hiding, only venturing forth when he could be certain of secrecy. At the time of Saint Nicholas' visit to my family, this was the situation still. Indeed, Old Nick himself had begun the new tactic of dressing as a caricatured copy of Nicholas: a fat, bearded, red-suited elf who lavishes expensive toys on selfish children who don't need them, stirring up the spirit of cupidity, and quenching the spirit of charity, in mockery of Nicholas' Christian work. It was for this reason that Cassiel had asked Nicholas to tell his story once a year, during Advent, that the truth might not be wholly buried under the avalanche of lies. And to my everlasting gratitude and joy, in the year of our Lord 1831, Nicholas chose my family to hear the tale.

As readers of this book must know, Old Nick has continued this deceitful strategy even in my own time, well into the twentieth century. Saint Nicholas the Christian minister has become an obese, cackling, gluttonous, secular myth. Yet know that when you see this Santa Claus, it is not the real Saint Nicholas, but Old Nick, the demonic Prince of Myra. But now, I see signs, subtle though they be, that Old Nick is trying a different tack: to destroy knowledge of Nicholas altogether, and with him, all belief in the Christmas Story. Such seems to me the path our society will take in the years to come, though it will likely take quite some time to get there. May God be pleased to block the path before we arrive at such a dark destination.

But what does all this mean? Has the noble Nicholas been defeated by his adversary, laboring for Christ in this world no longer? God forbid! It is true that the real story of Saint Nicholas has been gradually lost over the past hundred or hundred and fifty years. But the poems and stories written about him are at least partly true. Did Saint Nicholas really visit the houses of Christian families and secretly give presents on Christmas Eve? Yes, certainly. And he still does. But because of the false idol of Nicholas created by the Satanic Old Nick, the true Santa Claus can only continue this practice in the homes of those who know of his existence (and there were many more of those before the twentieth century). Even then, he gave his gifts in many different ways, as he always has: sometimes by leading a father or friend (without their realizing it) to find a desired gift; sometimes by whispering ideas for needed gifts that no one realized; sometimes by making and giving gifts himself. And sometimes, as if in courtesy to his own legend, he leaves his grace-gifts in children's stockings, as he once left bags of gold in the stockings of three fearful maidens in Myra. Even now, as he is of necessity somewhat more distant, he continues to work among the people of Christendom, that the celebration of Christ's nativity might be ever more glorious: helping parents find gifts for their children; helping the poor afford good gifts for their family; and many other kindly acts as well. His first ministry is, as it has always been, to the poor. But Nicholas' generosity finds its way into the homes of rich and poor alike, for the giving of gifts is a most excellent symbol of the Incarnation of Jesus Christ; and for this reason Nicholas specially loves the season of Christmas, with all its outpouring of gifts and kindness.

And so, many have thus encountered Saint Nicholas without knowing it, having heard his words spoken gently in their ears— so gently that they believed it was their own thoughts they were hearing—or having received gifts from others who unknowingly heard his words. Children find presents in their stockings and under their Christmas trees on Christmas morning. How came they there? Did Saint Nicholas pass by magic through the doors to leave those gifts to be found in the morning? Or did he whisper thoughts of generosity and love in the hearts of parents, guiding them, silently and invisibly, to find good gifts for their children?

Perhaps it is both of these. But always, with the work of Nicholas, howsoever he does his work, comes the whispered reminder of the story of Bethlehem: "It really is true, you know."

My last memory of that evening is of Mr. Nicholas, driving off into the night on a sledge—a sledge driven, nota bene, *not by horses, but by a sturdy brace of reindeer. Make of that what you will; but for my part, I must now end this tale. There is so much more I might say, but I cannot. I wanted to tell you how my father met Nicholas in the first place. It is a wonderful story. But my hand weakens so that I fear my penmanship will be but poorly legible to those who will read it. No more stories for old Jacob. Yet I must tell you that near the end of this little book, you will find a small copy of a painting my father did of Saint Nicholas. The original still hangs in my parlor. Father painted it from memory, for Nicholas would not sit for a portrait. Yet he captured Nicholas so clearly on his canvas, for his picture exactly matches my memory; except that no painting could ever quite capture the deep joy in the old man's eyes.*

No more of this. My eyes darken, and I know that death is near. And yet, I see through my window the beginning of the dawn, the dawn of Christmas morning. Surely, before the day, perhaps the hour, is out, I will see the face of my Savior, Jesus Christ, the greatest gift-giver, and the greatest gift; He to whom Nicholas of Myra is but a servant; for in comparison with our Lord Christ, Nicholas, as he himself would eagerly admit, is only a pale shadow. May Christ be honored by what I have written here, and may the work of Nicholas continue on to the glory of God.

One last word: if any in my family reads this account, please guard well the ancient manuscript I have enclosed. For on his deathbed, my Father told me that Old Nick himself, the Prince of Myra, in his guise as a scholar, has sought this document for hundreds of years, believing it to be a source of great power. For even the angels have their superstitions.

Jacob Reuel

25 December, 1925

That was the last written page in the book. Joshua turned to the back of the book, and there they found the portrait of Mr. Nicholas.

It was just as Jacob had described: the long white beard, the merry eyes, the scarlet cloak and hood. In one sense, he was very different from all the pictures of Santa Claus the children had seen in books, and on television, and billboards. But there was something also that was very familiar to them, and it wasn't just the white beard. If indeed the evil Old Nick was the source of all the commercialized portraits of Santa Claus, then the least that could be said was that Old Nick knew his subject well; and if the coal-in-stocking Santa, the North Pole Santa, was nothing but a caricature of the real thing, there yet remained something noble, and good, and magical, even in the caricature, that the wily Prince of Myra could not erase.

"Well, Joshua, what do you think?" said Rachel. "Can it be true?"

Joshua's eyes were still on the painted figure in the book. "I believe it *can* be," he said. "But I wish I knew if it *is*."

Part III: The Rescue

Chapter Fourteen

Superstition

It was time to leave, to go and meet Dad to get the Christmas tree. Rachel was about to place the book back on the shelf, but she hesitated; for just then they heard the whispering, page-turning ghost once more. Then she nearly dropped the book, struck with fear, as a voice screamed somewhere in the darkness of the room. From the opposite corner of the room, hidden behind the tree-like bookcases, the scream was followed by a noise as of someone falling, then running. Then a crash, as if the runner had struck against something in his flight. Then another, more horrible scream, and they could see a shadow, somewhat small, apparently, running toward the blue door; that door quickly opened, turning the shadow into a momentary silhouette; then the door banged shut, and all was silent again. Even the whispering had faded.

The children stood, frightened, and peered into the darkness to try to see what had happened, but they could make out nothing clearly. Joshua thought he saw another shadow moving slightly, just ahead of them on their left, but couldn't be certain. He stepped in front of his sister, one hand on hers; while Rachel wrapped her arms tightly around the book. For both children, after their initial moment of fright, and their instinctive desire to protect each other, had felt a strange and immediate urge to protect *the book*. And both were remembering, at the same moment, something from the book, some word or phrase near the end—what was it? Something about superstition? In their fear and uncertainty, they could not recall. But they could not shake the compelling feeling that they must, at all costs, *not* put that book back on the shelf. Instead...

"Let's take it to Mr. Tome ourselves," whispered Rachel, and Joshua nodded in agreement.

***

But what had just happened, and who had screamed? To understand that, we must go back more than an hour and a half: to the Library, just after Joshua and Rachel had left Father Lewis. Lou, the Guardian of Scientific Fact, the Dispeller of Myths, the Exposer of Fake Santas, had followed them out of the Library, bent on revenge. And he knew just how to get it: hearing the silly children and the sillier priest babble on about Santa Claus and Ghosts, Lou determined to follow Rachel and Joshua to the Old Page Bookshop, hide somewhere, and put on a little performance designed to scare the pants off these superstitious kids. He had to stifle a chuckle several times as he shadowed them. He couldn't wait to see their terrified faces. Lou had a trick of imitating the sounds of ghosts in a haunted house; it had served him well for scaring little kids, and had won him the respect of some of the bigger, meaner kids. He had perfected this part-whisper, part-moan, part-wail shtick, and was widely regarded, especially in his own mind, as a master. But he had never used it with the Kirk kids, so this was just perfect.

When he saw them hesitantly enter the alley, hand in hand, his scorn for them reached historic levels. He despised them, and hated them, and wanted more than anything else in the world, in that moment, to damage and scar them, to reduce them to shivering, weeping wretches. *That'll teach them to believe in fairy tales,* he thought, as if to assure himself that he was only acting out of the purest of motives. Then he followed them into the alley. Careful to keep out of sight and sound, he edged his way through the narrow, stuffy passage. They had looked back at him once, and he had been afraid then that they had seen him; but he ducked down, and they had gone on. But as the darkness grew, so did his uneasiness. *I don't like this: too closed in.* He was close enough to hear them talk about how they'd heard something. He listened closely and thought he heard a far-off voice. But he couldn't be sure. After Joshua and Rachel had passed through the wooden gate, he had been alone for some moments in the darkness, as he silently moved ahead. This place really, really bothered him, and a sense of panic started to swell and rise in his throat. *I've always been claustrophobic,* he reminded himself, for *of course* he was not bothered by thoughts of ghosts.

Finally, he reached the gate, and opened the icy doorknob, though he hated its image and shape. Peering around the edge of the door, he saw, after his eyes adjusted to the light, his two enemies just entering the bookshop. He remained outside for a few minutes, keeping the door cracked just enough to see them. He overheard their conversation with the owner, and his face burned with shame as heard the story of his father fainting in the shop—a story he'd never heard before, and which he angrily denounced in his mind as a lie. The thought of revenge grew sweeter by the moment.

Then, he slipped inside, sticking with them as they moved off to find the book. Or he *tried* to stick with them; but had to hide quickly once as someone else walked by. By the time he was able to come out again, he had lost them. He wandered in the store, then, trying to find the two children, for some ten minutes or so.

Lou didn't like this store at all. Ezra Tome's emergence from the back room had struck him like the appearance of some monster, and had given him, in that strange old place, a bad fright. He absolutely hated that shock of white hair. Lou's grandparents all lived far away, and he had not seen them since he was too young to remember it. And for a variety of reasons, mostly of the less-than-thoughtful sort, he had come to distrust older people; white hair, to him, was a sign of superstition, and evil, and so he had instantly recoiled when he first saw the shopkeeper.

Then there was the *oldness* of the place, especially of the books. Lou's house was very slick, sleek, polished, shiny, and modern: his mother made a point of replacing anything that accumulated even the slightest hint of age, or that lacked the light touch of current fashion. No grandfather clocks, antiques, or heirlooms graced his house, and he liked it that way. And as far as books, his mother read only magazines, and his father only new books. Even older works of a scientific nature were purchased in updated editions. His father's only concession to antiquity was a first edition of which he was somewhat proud, of a book published a hundred years before. Lou couldn't remember which book it was, but the date stuck with him because it was the only thing that old he had ever seen, having been published in 1859.

But this wretched bookshop was simply stuffed with old books, musty, dusty, ancient, old books; and while Lou's first reaction to this fact was contempt, this quickly changed to a kind of anxiety: what kind of people came here to read such old, outdated books? What might they do to him if they caught him? His skin began to crawl as he remembered things his father had told him about Medieval torture devices. And this looked just the sort of place to have something like that hidden away somewhere. He really, really, hated this old shop.

But what bothered him more than anything was the silence. This was evidently a place of study, of reflection, of thought; and, as Lou now realized, he was extremely uncomfortable with such things. At home, the television or radio was always on, and he carried a small transistor radio wherever he went. Even at night, he kept a radio running as he went to sleep. This deep quiet was unnerving, assaulting his ears worse than a deafening blast of trumpets; and he hated the silence as soon as he recognized it as the source of his uneasiness.

Now his mind began to half-consciously assemble all these elements—white hair, old books, silence—and to use them to build up a fear and hatred of this place that was only rivaled by his hatred of his grandmother's church, where they had been *forced* to go when she had died a year ago. As he edged through the shop, his abhorrence of the place went through several stages, clear and definable (though not to him): first, he filled up his soul with as much scorn and contempt as he could muster: this was a *silly* place, he thought to himself, silly, and weird and outdated. No one of intelligence would spend more than five minutes in such a place unless (like him) they had their own reasons for doing so.

But after a few minutes, his hatred began to take on a new form. His mind scurried, like a rat, over half-remembered bits of lore and legend and myth and mystery, over snatches of information he'd read in modern books of history, and scraps he'd picked up from the adult-like conversations in his home. His imagination began to conjure up images of Medieval Inquisitors and black dungeons; he dredged up vague ideas that he'd heard his father talk about, and which neither of them understood well: "religious oppression," "Crusader violence," and "bigotry and intolerance."

He worked these thoughts over in his mind until he had begun to think of The Old Page Bookshop as positively *dangerous*.

But even this complicated fear morphed and grew with each step he took until, his eyes darting back and forth and over his shoulder, his hands wringing in worry, the dark walls and high shelves and ancient writings becoming more and more ominous, he found himself at last on the edge of real terror. Indeed, he might have broken and run for it at last, if he hadn't at that moment found Joshua and Rachel.

A light ahead of him on his left had caught his attention, and he found himself at one of the two doorless entryways that led into the manuscript room. He remembered now his original purpose of scaring the two infants, and this helped him, for the moment, to forget that he himself was already quite scared. He crept in, through the rows of books, trying not to look up at the tree-like bookcases, until he found a spot only about twenty feet away, near the other corner, on the same wall as the Back Door. He thought he saw a light over to his left, near the back of the room, but either he had imagined it, or it went out immediately. He calmed his breathing and prepared to do the work for which he'd come.

But just then, Joshua had begun reading the book, and somehow Lou's interest was caught. He listened for a few minutes; then for a few minutes more. *It's the story of Santa Claus,* he realized. To his own irritation, he found he could not stop listening as Joshua read the story. And he knew exactly why: as the story unfolded, his mind, quite against his will, sailed back to a time years before. He was only a small boy, then, and he remembered, as Christmas neared, that he had happily told his father that he "can't wait for Santa Claus to come!" On hearing this, his father had turned on him in hot wrath, eyes blazing; for to that irreligious man, belief in Santa was no better than believing in the Tooth Fairy; or worse, in Christ Himself. After furiously denouncing his child's childish belief, his father had promptly laughed him to scorn, pouring such withering contempt on the boy that he had been afraid to speak to his father for a long time afterwards. Lou had cried himself to sleep that night, and woke the next morning, his soul purged entirely of belief in Santa Claus, imagination, magic, and, truth to tell, just about everything else.

He sat there in the bookstore, hidden by old books, and listening to Joshua read. And suddenly, a moment of perfectly clear choice presented itself to his mind: he could reject the anger that had driven him to become, like his father, a tormentor of those he despised. Or, he could embrace that anger, and turn it this way or that, even inward upon himself. For a few holy and magical moments, he saw and understood the choice, and considered it. It was his to make, and he made it. His soul seized the anger, holding it tightly, with silent promises of devotion. It was his anger, he had a *right* to it, he would keep it, and never—never—let it go. Lou had defined himself, before the eyes of everyone he knew, as a skeptic, a critic, a myth-buster; and his pride had invested too much in that image to lightly toss it aside.

But now the second choice: where to direct the anger? At his father? No, for that would make a mockery and a ruin of the life he had built for himself. Lou turned his eyes, and, at the same time, his anger, fully upon Rachel and her brother. The hate settled deeply into his soul and made itself comfortable there. And, in that moment, at least, he felt free, and happy. He became more determined than ever to hurt these foolish children any way he could, and his mind now began to consider this scare tactic only the beginning. New plans began to bubble up in the cauldron of his brain; with an effort, he turned away from them, preparing himself to begin the immediate work of terror that lay before him.

Now the story of Nicholas neared its end, and Lou puckered up his lips and put his hands to his mouth, in preparation for the sending forth of his dreadful ghost-sound. But before he could begin, another sound entered his ears: the sound of pages turning, and a voice whispering and muttering. It seemed to be coming from all around him. *Someone else is here,* he thought at first, and then (he couldn't keep the thought out of his mind), *someone who is not alive.* In an instant, full terror was upon him, and his only thought was to get away, to escape from the spirits. As he turned to run, he started in fright, for there before him was a very old, very frail, and very angry face: Old Cass was there, staring at him with all the wrath of a vengeful god, and Lou did not doubt in that moment that the elderly man (who he thought certainly was a ghost) had read his thoughts, knew his plans, and had come to carry him away to eternal torture.

Lou screamed and darted to his left and behind a tall bookcase, before careening into a table stacked with books. Several of these crashed to the floor, but he ran on unheeding, his breath rasping out in horror, his eyes bulging, his heart pounding. *Ghosts, ghosts, ghosts!* his mind screamed at him. All he wanted was to get out that door, but before he could reach it, he saw, just over to the side, a table that he didn't remember. It almost seemed to be glowing with an unearthly light. And sitting at the table was a man, dressed in clothes like they wore in the Dark Ages, he thought. And he was reading and whispering. *It's him, the ghost!* With another scream, Lou burst out the blue door, and then on until he was out of that horrible shop; and he kept running until he reached his home, where he collapsed into his mother's arms, sobbing and babbling of ghosts. His father was most disappointed.

Chapter Fifteen

The Rescue

After they heard Lou scream (though of course they didn't know who it was), Rachel and Joshua had decided not to place the book back on the shelves, but to deliver it personally to Mr. Tome. But they only took one step before Joshua touched his sister's arm, warning her by this to wait. Something else was moving in the room. Old Cass? If so, he was on a different side of the room, now, and was apparently hiding from them. It couldn't be him. Joshua nodded silently toward the shelves just to their left. Rachel saw it too.

"Let's go, quickly,' she said.

Too late. Out of the shadows between two tall bookcases, there emerged, silently, almost as if he had materialized out of the darkness that instant, a tall man. Rachel thought he looked familiar, but couldn't remember why. His head and face were completely hairless, not even the shadow of a shaved beard, and he wore thick glasses, a black overcoat, and a red and black tie. He was thin and pale, but surprisingly, the shape of his face suggested something of beauty and nobility: except for the glasses, Joshua thought he looked like an old Roman Caesar. Both children knew at once that they were in danger, though they were not certain why. Joshua tried to act normal, but his voice, when he spoke, came out in a bit of a squeak.

"Oh, hello," he said.

"Hello," said the man. His voice was deep and pleasant and almost hypnotic. "Is that *The Nicholas Book* you have there? I don't believe you can buy that."

"We know," said Rachel. "We're done with it now. We just need to take it back to Mr. Tome."

"I see. Actually, I need that book as well. I'm doing research for a book on Christmas customs and folklore, and I was told this old volume would be of great use to me. I'm Professor Princeton, a scholar of ancient customs, and…"

He hesitated, for he saw that these last words had had a profound effect on the children. But he continued, smiling as he spoke. "So if you don't mind, I'll take the book and save you the trouble of returning it."

Joshua was trembling, much more afraid now than he had been at the thought of ghosts. But he had to speak. *Here's where we find out how much danger we're really in,* Joshua said to himself. "No, thanks," he said out loud, and his voice cracked and wavered with fear. "We had a few questions to ask Mr. Tome about it. After that, I'm sure he'll be glad to let you see it."

That did it. The man reached somewhere inside his coat and pulled out a long, perfectly polished knife. The blade was curved like a scimitar, though it was only about as long as a Bowie knife. The handle gleamed gold in the candle fire, and the man's eyes seemed to darken as he pointed the blade right in the direction of Rachel's heart.

"The book," Professor Princeton said. "Set it down on the table, and then go."

The man took a step closer, fully out of the shadows now. In that moment of terror, Rachel experienced an unexpected rush of clarity, and as his face came clearly into view, she recognized him at last: he was the man on the ASL poster, the man at the library, the atheism lecturer, the face that had seemed so frightening to her, even in a photograph. He had obviously overheard their conversation and followed them here.

It was closer to the truth to say that he had followed Lou. Professor Princeton had seen at once that Lou was following the children as well, though he didn't know why. He had walked behind them, oblivious of the rain, for he never wore a hat or carried an umbrella. But he had kept pace with them until they entered the book shop. Finding it harder to slip inside than the smaller Lou, he had had to wait a bit longer, not wanting to be seen. When he finally got inside, the children were gone, and it took him some time to locate them. When he found them at last, Joshua was just beginning to read the book, and Old Cass had already gone, so the Professor did not see him. Yet he sensed that someone was nearby, and this had made him wary as he entered the manuscript room from the other open doorway, on the opposite side from where Lou was already hiding.

The Professor was after the book, of course. But as he heard Joshua begin to read it, he decided to bide his time. After all, he had overheard Father Lewis say that the book was not for sale; they would put it back when they were done and he could take it secretly, quietly, which he much preferred. But then, just when he was hoping to see the book safely replaced on the shelf, he had heard Lou scream. He had forgotten about the other boy, but he guessed at once who it was. He saw Lou run out the blue door. The Professor listened intently for any other sound. All was quiet. Perhaps the child had been frightened by ghosts. The Professor felt certain there *were* ghosts here: he could smell them. But the room seemed to be otherwise empty; though he was still slightly bothered by the sense that they were not quite as alone as he might have wished.

He made up his mind when he saw that the children now had no intention of returning the book to the shelf. There was small risk in an easy deception, so he stepped forward to request the book. But now that they had refused, he would have to take a harsher approach. He did not mind doing so, except that such encounters were almost always messy, inevitably causing as many problems as they solved.

"The book," he said again. "Set it down, and you will not be hurt."

"No, you can't have it!" Rachel's voice was defiant, despite her fear of this man. She held the book away from him, turning her shoulder as if to block him from taking it. Joshua stepped between them, almost numb with terror. His fists were clenched but he did not know what to do, or even what he *could* do. He briefly considered flinging a heavy book at the Professor's face, then making a dash for it with Rachel; but he knew there was a good chance that Rachel would be hurt in any sort of fight. He realized that the best way to protect her now was simply to give up the book. He was just about to have Rachel do so, when the Third Shadow emerged from behind a bookcase just behind and to the left of the Professor.

This Shadow was tall and hooded, and as it approached at an angle, they could see the silhouette of a big beard. Rachel and Joshua had the same thought at the same moment: *Saint Nicholas! Could it be?* But the only gift this Shadow brought was a hard punch to the Professor's jaw. The knife clattered against a table and then to the floor. The two men grappled and fought, but the Professor was evidently much stronger than he appeared, stronger than the Third Shadow, and he managed to get his hands on his knife again, and raised it to finish off his attacker. Just then the world exploded in painful light behind the Professor's eyes. Joshua had struck him hard on the head with the largest book he could find. The Third Shadow grabbed the Professor's knife hand and shouted. A moment later, the blue door burst open and Ezra Tome rushed in. The Professor leapt to his feet in wrath, tossing aside the Third Shadow as if he were a sack of straw, the Shadow crashing into a table of books. The Professor seemed almost like a giant in that moment, and it was clear to Rachel that there was no one in that room strong enough to stop him. He was just about to throw himself at Ezra Tome—and the children did not doubt that the shopkeeper would get the worst of that fight—when suddenly the Professor's eye seemed to catch something else in the shadows to his left. The children could not see what it was, but they saw the Professor's face twist into a sneer of hatred and fear; then, as if he knew he had lost the day, he turned and hurled himself against the green back door, which cracked, and burst off its hinges, flinging a shower of green splinters in its ruin. Before anyone could reach the back door, the Professor was gone.

Before another moment could tick by, a blur of movement launched itself from behind a bookcase, and shot past them, running after the Professor out the door. It took a few moments of bewilderment for the children to realize, with astonishment, that the runner was none other than the frail, elderly fellow who talked of Faerie: Old Cass himself!

There was a moment in which everyone was still; the only sound, the heavy breathing of Joshua and the Third Shadow. Cautiously,

Rachel picked up a candle from the table, and walked toward their fallen rescuer. Was it really Saint Nicholas? The Shadow was just raising himself from the broken table and scattered books where he had fallen. As he righted himself, the candlelight fell on his face. Then the children's jaws dropped almost as far as old Marley's had when he took off his bandage at Scrooge's house.

Rachel gasped. "Dad!"

Chapter Sixteen

Apples

Now, you might think that, having wondered if the Shadow was in fact Santa Claus, the children would be disappointed to find that it was only Dad, after all. But it was not so. Something had changed inside them throughout their adventures that day. And some of it only became clear to them later; but they were so filled with joy at the sight of their Father, that they found to their own surprise that they were actually glad, at least for the moment, that it was *not* Santa Claus. They both rushed to their Dad at once and pummeled him with such fierce hugs that he was knocked backwards into the wreck of the table once more.

Then there was laughter and more hugs and even a few tears all around. Dad was bruised and out of breath, but otherwise fine; he was more concerned for his little ones, who had just gone through a frightening and harrowing experience. Rachel was a bit shaken, but she was possessed of a great strength for bearing up under trouble and worry, and such healing as her soul required had already begun. Joshua was in fact elated, now that it was over, to have gone through such an adventure, and to have taken part, however small, in driving off the adversary. Later, he would find that the fear of that moment with the Professor would not so easily leave him; but for now, he was triumphant and happy.

Mr. Tome made a quick call to the police to report Professor's Princeton's attack and attempted thievery; then he retrieved a few more candles, and an oil lamp. And as everyone helped Mr. Tome fix up the fallen table and books, Dad told them the story of how he had come to be there. After the children had run into him on the street, he had noticed a strange man on a park bench nearby—a bald man wearing no hat against the rain. Dad had been seized by the conviction that this man was watching his children. He had gone back inside the store to avoid arousing suspicion, but had watched carefully from the window. Then he had clearly seen the Professor begin to follow them. And so Dad began to follow them as well. He soon saw that Lou was also following the children, and was struck by the strangeness of this merry little parade. *And a little child shall lead them,* he thought to himself. He followed them into the Old Page Bookshop, and kept close to Professor Princeton the whole time. Though he wasn't sure what might happen, he was deeply concerned about the intentions of this strange man who was shadowing his children. But being uncertain, he had also waited, and listened to Joshua read *The Nicholas Book* aloud. He guessed enough of what was going on: Father Lewis had sent them to the Old Page after a rare and curious book. Perhaps this man was a collector, and wanted the book for himself.

"In fact, that's exactly right," said Ezra Tome as he listened to Dad's story. "Professor Princeton is a collector of rare and valuable books, and especially manuscripts. And from what I've heard he's quite a ruthless collector. I've seen him in here before a time or two, though it's been a few years since he's been in town. He travels around the country, you see, giving lectures at Skeptic Societies, and researching rare books, and all that. Truth is, he did ask me once before about the Saint Nicholas book, wondering if I'd ever heard of it, but I didn't trust him; and the owner of the book had told me that not just anyone should be allowed to know about that book being here."

"Is that so?" said Father, rubbing his beard thoughtfully. "What I can't figure out is who ran after him. Must have been an Olympic racer, fast as he ran out that door."

"No, Dad, it was only Old Cass," said Rachel.

"Who?"

"Old Cass is a little old man who looks like he's about a hundred years old. How did he run so fast?"

"I don't know," said Mr. Tome. "That is remarkable, to be sure. There's always been something strange about Old Cass, though I've always liked him. I know almost nothing about him, really, except that he comes here every day I'm open and spends most of his time back here in the manuscript room. He's a real mystery."

"We thought that maybe..." Joshua hesitated. "Well, never mind." He looked hard at Rachel and she nodded. Both of them had their theories about Old Cass—and about the Professor—but they decided to keep quiet until they'd had more time to think it over.

Ezra Tome seemed to read more from their silence than they would have guessed. "I see you two are starting to connect some threads," he said. "And I won't tell you not to do it: this is a strange old shop, as I told you before, and unless I miss my guess, you two are wondering about some of the same things I've wondered about, too. But there are other possibilities, too, and we have to consider them."

"Like what?" said Joshua.

"Well, I've been thinking about the Anti-Superstition League, for one thing. After what happened to Ms. Track, I wouldn't be surprised if they've been keeping an eye out, and an ear, to find out what they can about my shop. If they somehow got wind of *The Nicholas Book,* they would have good reason to want to get their hands on it, either to expose it as just another ancient superstition— or to destroy it. Not only that, but Professor Princeton himself had a hand in starting the ASL over ten years ago."

"Did he really?" said Dad with raised eyebrows.

"He did, on one of his occasional visits to Bethlehem. That's one of the things he does: goes around and starts atheist clubs wherever he travels. So maybe he was acting on their behalf today."

"Could be," said Dad. "It's also rather interesting that Lou Nyten was here, his father being the president of the Anti-Superstition League."

"I wish I knew why he followed us," said Rachel.

"He was probably mad at what you said to him," said Joshua with a grin. "You really let him have it back at Wiseman's."

Rachel looked troubled. "I did kind of fly off the handle. But I guess The Old Page was a bit much for Lou. He probably heard William of Leyland turning pages and got scared."

"Perhaps his visit here will do him more good than it did his father," said Ezra. "But whether or not the ASL has a stake in this matter, I think it's more likely that the Professor just wanted to get his hands on a valuable book, and Old Cass, for some reason, felt it was his duty to stop him. He's always been a bit protective about *The Nicholas Book*. Don't know why, though perhaps Father Lewis can tell you more about it."

"Father Lewis?" asked Dad. "How does he fit in? I thought this was just an old book he'd read that he figured would be helpful to the children."

"No doubt he did, but there's more to it," replied the old shopkeeper. "You see, the owner of *The Nicholas Book* is none other than Father Lewis himself."

***

They left the Old Page Bookshop with much to think and talk about; but at first they did more thinking than talking. As they exited the shop, they looked up. The Magic Sky was now pouring a baptism of giant snowflakes on their heads—the first snow of the year. The children laughed and stretched their arms up to the Heavens. They bumped into things repeatedly, trying to keep their faces turned upwards as they walked. They headed back into town to get to Dad's car.

Snow fell on, and the sound of shoppers was nearly gone; it was almost 5:00, and most places were closed or closing. But Mr. Eden was about to roll his sidewalk fruit cart back inside his little grocery store. Dad gave him his last sale of the day by buying everyone apples. Rachel noticed a little flyer on his cart, announcing the Christmas play at Saint Augustine Church two nights hence. Mr. Eden thanked them, and rolled his cart inside, while the three adventurers moved on down the street. On the way, they passed Town Hall, right in the center of town, at the crossing of Stable Road and Star Street. The heavy clouds and approaching twilight made the sky almost dark, but the lawn of the Bethlehem Town Hall was bright, for there it was: the Town Crèche, the Nativity scene. Hand-carved and painted more than half a century ago by an artist, it looked much more real than the plastic, mass-produced substitutes one too often sees on City Lawns. The light came from tastefully-placed electric lamps, set for illumination rather than spectacle.

"Wait, Dad," said Rachel, when she saw it. Joshua had already stopped, his eyes fixed on the painted and carved moment, a flash of history. It was indeed more historical than most Nativities, showing the Wise Men far to the right (the East, in fact), gazing up at the Star (hung from the branches of an overhanging tree) and pointing, rather than kneeling, by the Shepherds, as in the less-than-historical plastic Nativities.

The world was quiet, and seemed to be listening, or waiting. A church bell chimed the hour, and Dad smiled; he knew it must be Saint Augustine Church, for only Father Lewis insisted on ringing the hours, throughout the year, reminding the people that all time was God's time. Somewhere closer by, they could hear the voices of a church choir, rehearsing for a Christmas service. *Glory to the newborn King.*

They stood in silence for some while, even their apples forgotten. It was quiet here, and all three reveled in the absence of clamor. Then they began to talk about the Christmas story itself: imagining what it must have been like to have been there, to have been forced to choose whether or not to believe that your neighbor had just given birth to the Son of God. In many ways, they realized, faith was just as hard back then as it was now. But the world was just as full of reasons to believe as it ever had been; perhaps more so.

"Dad, I was just thinking," said Joshua.

"What's that?"

"This," and he pointed to the crèche, "this *is* Christmas. Saint Nicholas knew that. And I was thinking about what he did at the Council of Nicaea."

"Yes?"

"Well, I was thinking of all the kids at Wiseman's, and I was wondering what Saint Nicholas would do if he saw all this attention being given to him instead of Jesus."

"And what do you think he would do?"

"I think he would punch somebody!"

They all laughed at that. The cold air stung their faces, but it seemed pleasant, and they had no desire to go. But eventually, they all seemed to sense that the time for departure was at hand. All the questions that still burned in their minds, their eager anticipation of the conversation they knew they would have later that night, their memory of the adventure they had just gone through—none of these seemed all that important while they were standing there in the snow, pondering Christmas.

"This is the real magic, Dad," said Rachel.

Joshua nodded and smiled. "I think we've just created a new First Day of Holiday Tradition." He took a bite of his apple, as the magical fire kindled in their hearts.

Dad had kneeled down between his two children, with his arms around them. Glancing at his face, Rachel suddenly took a tuft of his beard in her hand and gave it a sharp yank.

"Ow!" said Dad, with a wince of pain, as Rachel giggled. "What was that for?"

She smiled as she said, "It's real." Dad burst out laughing.

Chapter Seventeen

The Tree

After getting the car, they drove several miles out of town, traveling south, until they reached a long road with lakes and rolling hills on either side.

As they drove, Joshua and Rachel were both pensive and quiet. There were many things they wanted to ask their father. Joshua, running through the dozen questions in his head, selected one, almost at random, to get the conversation started.

"Dad," he began, "the book said that Nicholas was the leader of the *longaevi*. I sort of remember that word, from an old book of yours, I think. What does it mean?"

"Well, it means 'long-livers.' It was the Medieval word for Elves, or Faeries."

"But aren't they a different sort of Faeries? I mean, they're not like Mustardseed and all those from *A Midsummer Night's Dream,* are they?"

"No, that's right: closer to Oberon and Titania, really. No butterfly wings or antennae. These were *Elves,* but not the silly little workshop elves you see in all the modern stories about Santa. These were the Long-Livers of Medieval tales, fierce, and proud, and beautiful, and...*tall*." He chuckled. "These Elves would probably scare young Lou as badly as the ghosts did. No one ever dreamed of laughing at a real Elf."

"So they're kind of like the Elves in those books we read last year, right?"

"Which ones?"

"The Lord of the Rings."

"Yes, exactly. I hope Professor Tolkien has a few more like that up his sleeve. But yes, that's just the kind of Elves I mean. One difference you'll notice is—ah, we'll have to finish talking later. Here we are—the Call Tree Farm."

Mr. Call and his family had run this place for many years, and the annual trip to cut down one of the fine Call trees had been a Kirk family tradition for the past five years. But this year the tradition was to end: Mr. Call was retiring, and this was the last year he would keep his Christmas tree farm in operation.

"Well, let's go," said Dad, a little sadly, as they parked in the long gravel driveway. "One last tree from Mr. Call, eh?"

There was a placid pond on their left, and a large, inflatable snowman in the yard near the house. A little, ornate bench sat nearby. They walked through the driveway to their right, and gazed out on the acres of evergreens before them. Fraser Firs, White Pines, and Leyland Cypresses awaited the visitors. Fresh cut Christmas wreaths were hanging up near the little barn down the hill. Mr. Call and his daughters were helping a couple of other customers. Dad smiled. The quietness of this secluded farm always drew him in and haunted him for weeks afterward. Along with the Christmas Eve service at church each year, this day, the Day of the Christmas Tree, more than anything else, really *felt* like Christmas.

The air was sharp with the young winter touch, and the snow still fell on. There was a wooden post near the driveway, and on this was hung several sharp handsaws. There were also several ribbons of various colors, each with a price beside it. For the cost-conscious, all that was needed was to remember the ribbon color or two within one's price range, and watch for them while looking through the trees. Dad selected his saw, and lightly fingered the blade. "Mr. Call always keeps 'em sharp!" he said. He pulled on some gloves, and they went out to find Their Tree.

For the next half hour they walked happily through rows and rows of trees, trying to find the perfect tree for the Kirk Christmas. As they walked and pondered, Rachel was struck by a strange sense of familiarity—not the familiarity of past years in this same place, but something new and different: this place, so old as a stronghold of their own family lore and tradition, now stirred memories of something else, something recent, something she could not quite place. But the memories kept elbowing her mind until finally, as she stood with her father and brother in a long, even row of the taller Leyland Cypresses, it came to her. The trees loomed above her, and she stretched her neck upward to see their tops. The trees towered over her like...like...

Like bookcases. At the Old Page Bookshop she had felt the same odd sense of memory, but could not fit it into its proper place. Now she knew: the bookcases had reminded her of these trees; now, the trees reminded her of the tree-like bookcases. The tallest one of the bunch caught her eye: it seemed to sparkle with its ornamental snow crystals, and stood proudly, perfectly formed and symmetrical. She leaned closer to it, reaching out her hand to touch its soft, yet prickly branches. Her eyes seemed to shift, somehow, and for a single moment, the Tree really looked like a bookcase. And it occurred to her that a Bookcase was precisely what it was: all trees were leafy libraries, woody words, spoken by their Maker. And a Christmas Tree was doubly so, having one particular Story to tell, with the voices of Angels, Shepherds, and Magi whispering among its leaf-pages; its glowing lights flashing with the Story of the Light of the World. She'd had a second cousin whose family didn't celebrate Christmas, and considered a Christmas tree nothing more than a pagan bush. She found this hard to understand: how could a Tree, made by God, and bearing symbols of the Light of the World, say anything to the world except, "Hear the True Story of Bethlehem"?

"This one, Daddy. I'm sure of it."

Dad and Joshua walked all around the tree several times, looking it over closely.

"Yeah, I like it too," said Joshua.

"It is a beauty," agreed Dad. "Bit tall, though. Might have to chop a bit off the top to make it fit in the living room."

"No," said Rachel with conviction. "It'll fit."

The tree was out of the price range Dad had had in mind, but somehow the adventures of that Day seemed to demand a special sacrifice. He nodded, and knelt down to begin sawing. Joshua had always helped a little, but for the last couple of years, he'd been big enough to actually make a difference, so he took his turns at the saw. He also took a few symbolic swings with his little hatchet, a beloved tool he'd been given by his grandparents a few years before.

"Young Jethro swung his mighty axe!" quoted Dad, and they all laughed. He said the same thing every year; yet the ritual never became ritualistic. A few minutes later, the trailblazing saw pushed through the bark on the other side of the trunk, a path to the West opened at last.

"Timber!"

So the Christmas Tree fell, beginning the slow giving of its life to bring light and joy for the coming mingled fortnight of Advent and Christmas. At the end of that time, it would be carried with reverence and solemnity to the Christmas Tree Graveyard, just past the edge of the woods outside the Kirk house; there it would have the year of its own advent carved at the base of the trunk, and be bidden a fond, grateful farewell.

Dad and Joshua carried the tree over to the barn. There was a warm fire blazing in a large, rusty, metal barrel. The sun had sunk behind the hills: twilight was upon them, and the fire shone heat and beauty in the grey evening. One of the Call ladies chain-sawed an inch or so off the bottom of the trunk to even it out; then Mr. Call put the tree on his "shaking machine," as Joshua called it, and shook out the loose needles. "This is to shake out any squirrels, snakes, possums, or coons," said Mr. Call, with a smile deeply carved in his sun-browned face. "Hey, watch out there!" Suddenly, something small and gray shot out from the branches of the tree. Rachel knew it was coming but couldn't suppress a small shriek that quickly resolved into laughter. It was a stuffed squirrel. Joshua smiled. If he'd seen a quick flick of Mr. Call's wrist just before the squirrel jumped out of the tree, he never mentioned it.

Mr. Call then netted the tree in a baler, while his daughter gave candy canes to the children. He and Dad talked about how the Christmas tree business was faring that year, and Dad told the revered tree farmer how much they would miss the old place. Mr. Call allowed as how he would miss a lot of things, too, now that it came to it. He offered a homemade Christmas wreath, and, the price seeming fair, Dad accepted.

Mr. Call carried the tree over to the family car, a 1948 Ford Woodie station wagon. He tied it to the top, and then, all too quickly, it was time to go. Dad and Mr. Call shook hands, and Dad offered hearty thanks for Mr. Call having been such a vital part of the family Christmas, lo, these many years. The children also said their thanks, and gave Mr. Call a batch of Christmas cookies that Mom had made earlier that day just for him and his family.

As they drove down the long driveway for the last time, Dad was silent and meditative. So were the children, but for different reasons, perhaps. For Dad it felt like the end of an era. His first trip to the Call Tree Farm five years ago still stood out in his mind as one of the great days of his life. He had only taken Joshua that year, and they had connected as Father and Son in a new way that afternoon, cutting down their Christmas tree with their own hands. He sighed, but recalled something from C.S. Lewis about how a joy is never full until it is experienced as a memory. He smiled, and turned on the radio. Bing Crosby's Christmas musical story, *How Lovely is Christmas*, was just starting. They had caught it every year so far, and it was as much a part of their tradition as cutting down the tree. Indeed a young boy chopping down a tree with a magical axe was a key part of the story. Dad looked back at his two children, and thanked God for the magic of these two treasures, and for the tree that rode the wind on the top of their car. He almost felt as if the car were flying, as if the Story-Tree were driving *them* home.

Chapter Eighteen
The White Lady

As Ford Woodie headlights turned into the driveway, Marian Kirk, better known to our two young protagonists as Mom, glanced out the dining room window and smiled. The voice of Nat King Cole, captured magically in vinyl, had just finished singing *The First Noel* several minutes ago, ending the record, but she had not yet put anything else on. She walked into the living room and opened the cupboard doors where their stacks of Christmas records had been stashed for the season. *The Carrying Home of the Christmas Tree calls for something special,* she said to herself. With this as her standard, she selected Bach's *Christmas Oratorio,* and put it on the turntable. It was a new recording, only released the year before, and recorded in St. Thomas Church in Leipzig, one of the two original churches (the other being the church of St. Nicholas) where the great music had first been performed more than two hundred years before.

Mom re-lit one of the candles that had gone out, straightened a few pillows, picked up a couple of stray toys, then poured fresh hot chocolate into three red and green mugs. She popped several marshmallows and a candy cane (for stirring) into each cup, and waited. She heard no sound from outside. Were they coming in? She glanced out and saw no movement. Apparently everyone was still sitting in the dark car. Talking, perhaps?

Two of her youngest children, John and Anna, came into the kitchen, smelling the chocolate and hoping to partake. She smiled and poured two more cups of hot chocolate. She walked down the hall to check on Elizabeth, their nine-month-old baby, who was still sleeping; then she settled into her chair, her eyes involuntarily closing. She was weary, and her arms and legs ached. But it was a joyous sort of weariness; and even though she looked forward to the restfulness of sleep, the tiredness itself was a kind of pleasure. She loved her calling and was very good at it. She regarded that calling as a kind of art.

Outside, the children and Dad had sat in the car, quiet and still, after Dad turned off the engine. They had much on their minds. The children each had a small army of questions fighting for the front of the line in their heads, but none emerged as clear victors, so Rachel and Joshua remained silent.

"Well," said Dad after a few minutes. "We have a lot to talk about—that book, especially—but I think the Supper Table is the best place for it. What do you say?"

"Sounds good to me, Dad."

"Me too."

"One other thing," continued their Father. "Your Mom has done a lot of work to make tonight special, and I don't want her worried about anything. So not a word about what happened at the book shop. I'll tell her later myself. Understood?"

"Yes, sir," came the reply.

"All right, then. Go ahead in. I'll get the tree."

The children walked to where the side door, their main entrance, sat atop a small porch accessed by three brick steps. Snow was still falling, and Rachel felt a thrill of joy as each flake fell on her or the porch or the ground or her brother. The world seemed a new place to her; things she walked by without noticing in the past now beckoned her eyes to their beauty: the world was baptized with white, but this seemed somehow to accentuate the true color of everything. Was it because white was somehow a blend of all colors? She almost felt the greenness of the trees, even though it would be some months before she would see it again. Beauty surrounded her like a cloud of glory, passing through her and into her, filling her with light and life and joy.

Joshua felt it too, though for him the world now seemed to present itself to his eyes as one majestic gift, beautiful and terrible, full of sound and fury, signifying everything. The key note struck in his heart by the world's music was gratitude. He felt, perhaps for the first time, thankful to be alive, in the world, in the world's story. He knew himself for a character in that story. He had to say "thank you" to someone, or he would burst. He closed his eyes, whispering his thanksgiving to the Storyteller, the crafter of his character.

Why did they feel this way? They hardly wondered at the time, though later they thought that perhaps it was just the relief of having survived an encounter with that cruel, curved knife—and its owner, who, they were convinced, was much more dangerous than he appeared. But Joshua later came to believe that the truth of the matter was something more, something Old Cass had hinted at back at The Old Page.

Joshua opened the door. A wave of delicious smells struck their faces: chocolate and cinnamon, and those scented candles Mom liked to use. The light from inside momentarily blinded them: as they focused, they saw that all the normal lights were out, but Mom had strung white Christmas lights around the living room and kitchen, and lit candles everywhere. To the children, it seemed as if the door to Faerie Land had been opened, and they wondered how they could ever have thought the plastic castle at the Department Store beautiful compared to this.

They walked through the doorway, and entered the place of magic. Their eyes were still adjusting to the light, and for a few moments, they could discern nothing clearly. Then, Rachel gave a little gasp, for there, just ahead of them in the kitchen, they saw a very great Lady. She was fair and tall, and her golden hair lay long upon her shoulders. There was a light in her eyes, brighter than the Christmas lights and the candle fire, and a great smile was on her face. She was robed in flowing garments of white; and white light seemed to shine from her. Who was it? Perhaps they *had* gone into Faerie Land after all, and here was the Faerie Queen herself! Joshua and Rachel were both struck with a strong urge to kneel to the Lady; instead, they rushed to her, arms open wide, for in a moment they knew her: the Great Queen was their own Mother. The momentary glimpse of glory faded, and the white garments became a simple apron and dress.

"Mom!"

"We're home!"

The music of the mighty Bach filled their ears, and here was yet another new beauty: they had heard the music before, but once again, they heard it now as if it were newly composed, as if they were hearing it in the great church of St. Nicholas in Leipzig, the first of millions of hearers. Mom took their hands and led them to the counter where their cups of hot chocolate waited. The children sipped them, but in their happiness, a thread of concern wove itself into their minds. They glanced at each other in silent agreement and nodded. Then, at the same moment, they both began talking, thanking, and asking, almost pleadingly, what they could do to help. They were both filled with the sudden and certain conviction that they must serve this great Lady, at once, that she must do no more work today. She laughed and wondered at this strange plot twist, but gratefully consented. They bade her sit down, and made her a cup of hot chocolate.

Then a noise at the door turned all their heads. Dad was coming in with the tree. And here again the children's eyes saw him as if for the first time: the bearded, hooded man, carrying a tree on his shoulders, now seemed a King of Elves, as magical to them as flying reindeer. They turned at another noise in the kitchen. Mother had escaped from the recliner and was checking the cookies in the oven. *Yes,* thought Rachel, and Joshua's thoughts were much like hers. Their Mother truly was a Faerie Queen, more enchanting than a hidden snow-kingdom.

They helped Dad get the tree in and up, and Joshua poured some water from a green watering can. Rachel had been right: it was a perfect fit. She began setting the table, and Mom opened the first box of ornaments.

"Supper will be ready soon," Mom said. "Oh, and Rachel, set an extra plate and silverware. We're having a guest tonight."

"We are?" said Rachel. "Who's coming?"

"Didn't you tell them, Dear?" said Mom, turning to Dad, who was eyeballing the tree, which he still thought was not quite straight.

"No, I thought I'd wait and let them be surprised. But I guess it's okay to tell them now. He'll be here any minute, anyway."

"Then who is it?" said Joshua.

"Father Lewis."

Chapter Nineteen

Supper

Father Lewis arrived about three minutes later, a thick layer of snow on his black coat and hat—quite a lot, considering he had only walked from the driveway to the door. But the snow was falling large and fast, now. After a bit more hot chocolate and some laughing welcomes and small talk, everyone settled down to supper.

Supper was breakfast, a Kirk family specialty, occasionally served for the evening meal. There was bacon and sausage, eggs and grits, hash brown potatoes, biscuits and cheese, lots of fruit, and all topped off with a built-in dessert (which most chose to have *with* the meal), pancakes. It was a glorious feast, and the children would recall it afterwards as one of the best meals of their childhood. But they were hungry for something more than food. And it was obvious to most everyone at the table that quite a bit of talking was called for.

"And," said Mom, "I want you all to start by telling me what happened today. It's obvious that you've all had some sort of adventure, and I want to hear it. *All* of it." This last sentence was spoken with a glance at Dad, who was looking just a bit anxious. It was clear that Mom knew her family too well for Dangerous Quests and Exploits to pass her notice, whatever promises of silence had been made in cars before coming in.

"Of course, Marian," said Dad. "And with Father Lewis coming over, I figured Supper would be the best time to tell you, since part of it involves him. And yet there are some parts of it that even he doesn't know, yet."

Then they told the story of their day: Joshua and Rachel began with what happened at Wiseman's with Lou and the Department Store Santa. They followed the tale until the Library, where Father Lewis put in a bit of commentary. Then Dad picked up where he met the children in the street. And from there, everyone piped in until the story was told. Father Lewis was certainly interested in what happened at the Old Page Bookshop with Professor Princeton and Old Cass, though Dad thought he wasn't all that surprised. And while Mom's hand went to her mouth several times, and her face got paler as she heard how her children had been followed and accosted—Dad told that part of the story with as much care and tact as he truthfully could—she remained calm, though she squeezed Joshua's hand tightly (he was closest to her) and did not let it go for some time.

"Well, that's quite a tale," she said when it was over, her voice quivering only very slightly. "Frightening, really: more frightening, perhaps, than you children realize."

"More frightening for the two parents, I think," said Father Lewis with a smile.

"But you are all right, and all is well," she said in a voice rich with gratitude.

"God be praised," said Dad.

"God be praised," said Mom and Father Lewis.

"Yet something doesn't seem quite right," said Mom. "Why on earth would the Professor *follow* Joshua and Rachel from the Library? Wouldn't he rush ahead to get the book before them?"

"I thought about that, too," said Dad. "But I think his plan makes sense, after all. Ezra told us that the Professor had inquired about the book some years ago; now, finding that it had been at The Old Page all along, he must have realized that Ezra had purposefully kept that fact from him, and therefore that some measures were being taken for its security. Also, he had no idea where the book might be located in the shop. It's a big place. But by following the children, he could find out exactly where the book was, and quietly steal it after they left."

"That makes sense," said Father Lewis. "I think you're right, Joseph."

"But now," said Dad, "I believe there are a few other questions that want answering. And do not imagine that it was for his fine and desirable company alone that I was compelled to invite this good priest to the Kirk home this evening. From what Ezra Tome told us today, Father Lewis here holds the secret to all our questions."

"To some of them, anyway," said the priest. "I suppose you want to know about *The Nicholas Book?*"

"Yes, please!" said Rachel.

"Very well, then. You know that the book was written by a man named Jacob Reuel in 1925. What you do not know is that Jacob Reuel was my great grandfather."

The children's mouths dropped open, and Joshua's fork clattered on his plate.

"He was?" This was spoken by both the twins, at the exact same moment, causing Father Lewis to laugh.

"Yes, he was. He died when I was in my late twenties. But I never knew about the book until my father died about seven years ago. I found it among his belongings then."

"He never told you about it while he was alive?" said Mom.

"No."

"That seems strange."

"Perhaps. But even if Dad did read Grandpa Jacob's story, he would not have believed it."

"Why not?" asked Rachel.

"Because Jacob Reuel was a novelist: he wrote stories for a living."

"Jacob Reuel," said Dad. "I don't believe I've ever heard of him."

"Well, that's not surprising, really. Grandpa Jacob was a *failed* novelist: none of his books ever sold well, and he never made much money as a writer."

"But he was a writer, all the same," said Rachel, "so does that mean everything he wrote about Saint Nicholas was just a made-up story?"

"Maybe. But not necessarily. For one thing, I found a rather mysterious reference in Grandpa Jacob's diary that seems to be about the twelfth-century manuscript mentioned in *The Nicholas Book.*"

"We were going to ask you about that," said Joshua. "The manuscript was not in the book."

"But there was a leather pouch in the back," added Rachel. "We thought it might have been made to hold the old manuscript."

"That may be," said Father Lewis. "But I cannot say for certain, since I have never seen the manuscript. It was not in the book when I first found it, and though I have searched diligently for it, I have been unable to locate it."

'That's disappointing," said Dad. 'So, no trace of it at all?"

"Well, maybe."

"Oh?"

"In my search for the manuscript, I did find, among Grandpa Jacob's papers, a small scrap of old vellum. That's a very fine sort of calfskin parchment. It was only a small scrap, no bigger than your fingertip. I had it looked at by a friend of mine who specializes in old writing, and he says it dates back from the Middle Ages." He paused a moment, and looked hard at both Joshua and Rachel. "And very possibly from the twelfth century."

Joshua smacked his hand on the table, missing, unfortunately, the reproving look his Mother gave him. "Then that proves it, right?"

"Perhaps. Perhaps not. I'd feel more certain about the whole thing if I could lay my hands on the actual manuscript, though."

"I wonder what happened to it," said Joshua. "Maybe Jacob hid it, to make sure Old Nick never found it?"

"Possibly."

"So then you don't...you don't think the story your Grandpa Jacob told is true?" said Rachel.

"Well, I didn't say that. It is possible, of course, that he made it all up, including the so-called "translation" of the older manuscript in his book: just an added touch of authenticity for his little Santa Claus story."

"Is that what you think happened?" asked Mom.

Father Lewis smiled, and swallowed a mouthful of apple cider before continuing. "Not really," he said at last. "I can't be sure, of course, but I think it very likely that this was *not* one of Grandpa Jacob's fictional stories. For one thing, he never wrote in the first person like that: always said he disliked that sort of writing, though I never understood why."

"Yes, it seemed as if he were recounting something that really happened to him," said Dad. "Even down to the shaky handwriting, which one would expect of a man of a hundred and three."

"Or a hundred and four!" chimed in Joshua, who had a little too much bacon in his mouth for proper conversation.

"That's true," said Father Lewis. "And that's connected to another reason I don't really think this was an attempted novel. You see, Grandpa Jacob really *was* born on Christmas Eve, and he really *did* die on Christmas Day, 1925, the very date he wrote in this book."

"Then..." said Rachel, her pulse quickening, "then what he wrote is true?"

"Well, I didn't say that, either," said the priest. "There are a few possibilities: either everything he wrote is true, and he really did meet the immortal Saint Nicholas back in his childhood; or he made it all up, including the story of the Medieval Nicholas manuscript, in one last attempt to write a successful book before he died; or maybe he *thought* he was telling the truth about a man who was *not* Saint Nicholas, after all."

"What do you mean?" asked Joshua.

"I mean, maybe he really did meet an interesting old man with wild tales to tell. And as a child, he might have mistakenly thought this man was the one and only Saint Nicholas, Santa Claus himself."

"Santa Clock!" said two-year old Anna. Everyone laughed, except Father Lewis, whose attention to a bite of hash brown potatoes only allowed him to smile.

"But," said Dad, giving his old mentor a piercing look, "that's not what you think, is it?"

A napkin passed over Father Lewis' mouth before he continued. "No," he said. "None of that rings true to me. But that's as far as I can go, in any case. I have my views on the matter, but I cannot say with full certainty whether old Jacob's story is true or not." They fell to silent thought, but Rachel was thinking about the two stories that seemed to weave together in all that had happened that day: the stories of Christ and of Saint Nicholas. "How do we put these two stories together?" she asked.

"We've seen a good example of the difference only today," said Father Lewis. "Think of it this way: we know Christ crossed back from death to life the same way we know Caesar crossed the Rubicon, or Washington crossed the Delaware: historical records. This *Nicholas Book* of Grandpa Jacob's is different, however: it may be true, but we have real questions about *why* it was written. But there is no question about why the New Testament was written: the writers told us. They wrote to set down in writing the things they had seen and heard. And remember that this was long before anyone thought of writing historical fiction. We have a great deal of certainty about the birth of Jesus in Bethlehem. We can't be *quite* as certain about the Saint Nicholas legend."

"There are other things I still don't understand," said Mom. "Like why you put *The Nicholas Book* in Ezra Tome's bookshop, and what this mysterious Old Cass has to do with it."

"Yes, and who *is* Old Cass?" said Joshua. "And Professor Princeton? We thought—Rachel and I thought—well..." He fell silent, feeling a bit shy about his theory now that it came to expressing it.

"It's all right, Joshua," said Rachel. "Tell them."

"Well," began Joshua, "We thought that maybe...maybe Professor Princeton was Old Nick himself."

"Right," said Rachel. "The manuscript did say Old Nick wanders around disguised as a scholar. *And* that he was after the twelfth century manuscript."

"That's quite a thought," said Mom. "But then what about Old Cass?" But she thought she already knew what they would say.

"We were thinking about that, too," said Joshua, excitedly. "If the Professor really is Old Nick, then who is Old Nick's great enemy?"

"Huh," said Father, impressed by this line of thinking. "Cassiel the angel."

"Exactly!" said Rachel with wide eyes. "The name even fits: Cassiel. Old Cass!"

"Yep, that's what I was thinking," said Joshua. "But what do *you* think about all this, Father Lewis?"

"Ah, well, I can answer some of that," replied Father Lewis. "When I found the book seven years ago, I was of course fascinated by it. I showed it to an acquaintance of mine, the man you know as Old Cass."

"Why him?" said Rachel.

"I told you that my great-grandfather's books never sold well in his lifetime. But after he died, his books finally became popular... sort of. They became what we might call "cult classics:" that is, they became fashionable as novelty books with a small and devoted readership. Jacob Reuel Societies sprang up all over the country, and even overseas. His books had always been published with small print runs, and as a result, were now rather rare. Thus they became collector's items, selling for many thousands of dollars. I had met Old Cass a time or two, here and there, and found him an interesting character. He'd come to my church a few times, and I had run into him at the Old Page Bookshop, too. Well, it turned out he was a great fan of Grandpa Jacob's books, or..." The priest hesitated, considering his words. "Or, at least, he knew a lot about them. So I thought he might be interested in Jacob's last book, whether true or fiction.

"He was indeed most interested, and seemed to attach a great deal of importance to the book. And it was he who encouraged me to place the book in Ezra's store, but not for sale: just as a curiosity for those who might be interested. I was hesitant to do so, because I knew that book collectors can sometimes be rather a cutthroat lot, and I was afraid it might be stolen. But he said he'd keep an eye on it. You might think I would laugh at the idea of this ancient man protecting the book from ruthless collectors, but if you've known Old Cass as long as I have, you wouldn't think that way. He's...well, he's a remarkable fellow."

"We noticed," said Joshua, and Rachel and Dad nodded.

"So," continued Father Lewis, "I agreed. And there the book has sat ever since. I've gone back a time or two to read it again, but hardly anyone else has ever looked at it, from what Ezra tells me. But when I heard today that you had questions about Saint Nicholas, of course my first thought was to have you read it."

"But Father Lewis," said Rachel, "who *is* Old Cass? And Professor Princeton? Your great-grandfather's book said that Old Nick, the fallen angel who was Saint Nicholas' great enemy, wanted to find that old manuscript because he thought it would give him great power."

"Yes, I remember," said Father Lewis. "'Even the angels have their superstitions.'"

"Superspishum is bad!" said four-year old John.

"Yes, very bag!" said Anna, with a look of grave concern on her face.

Baby Elizabeth laughed and shook her head, her signature expression for the past three weeks. Rachel smiled. "Anyway, that's an exact description of Professor Princeton. He wanders around, looking for old books, pretending to be a scholar!"

"Ah, but which book was he looking for?"

"He told us," said Joshua. *"The Nicholas Book."*

"But which one?"

"The...what do you mean?"

"Remember, there are possibly *two* books: the twelfth century manuscript, and the 1925 book written by my great-grandfather. The only copy of Jacob Reuel's last story—handwritten by the author, at that—would likely sell for enough money to make someone rich. Maybe Professor Princeton was after that. Or maybe he is indeed some physical manifestation of an evil spirit, out to fight against the true Saint Nicholas, and to retrieve the ancient book that told the story of his life.

"As to Old Cass, it is strange that his name is so similar to the angel Cassiel. But in truth, I never thought about it, since I knew Old Cass before I ever read Grandpa Jacob's book. Old Cass is a remarkable and mysterious old man, and I often feel that he is either much older, or much younger, than he appears. I never can decide which it is."

"So let me see if I have this right," said Mom. "The evil angelic power, the so-called Prince of Myra, better known as Old Nick, thinks the manuscript telling the story of Nicholas' life is some sort of magic talisman, a source of great power. And he thinks, perhaps with good reason, that the manuscript is tucked into the back of *The Nicholas Book.*"

"But it wasn't," said Rachel.

"True, but Old Nick may not have known that. After all, the book did contain a translation of the manuscript, and Old Nick, if that's who he is, may have learned that the manuscript had come into Jacob's possession. But if it's true, and if Jacob was right that Old Nick's belief in the manuscript's power was only an angelic superstition, then what is Old Cass doing there, and why is he, apparently, guarding the book?"

"Perhaps because it is worth guarding, after all," said Father Lewis. "As is every good story."

"Or maybe," said Dad, "as a strategy to draw Old Nick into the open."

"That's a thought," replied the priest. "If so, then Cassiel was actually hunting for his ancient enemy, drawing him into battle. But there is one more chapter in this tale, which may answer your question a bit better." He swallowed another sip of cider, then continued. "About an hour and a half ago, I was back at the church, writing my sermon. I felt odd, suddenly, as if someone were watching me. I looked up and realized I had a Visitor, right there in my study: Old Cass.

"He had come, he said, to let me know that an attempt had been made to steal my great-grandfather's book. He told me then the story of what happened to you children this afternoon."

"Ah," said Dad. "I thought you looked as if you already knew the story."

"Yes, well, Old Cass also told me that he had pursued the Professor, but had not been able to capture him. He wanted to warn me that the Professor would likely make another attempt, 'now that he knows where the book is,' he said. Evidently, the Professor has been looking for the book for a long time."

"But as you said," Rachel added, "which book?"

"The twelfth-century manuscript, according to Old Cass; *not* Jacob Reuel's book. I wondered at that, and some thoughts began to form in my mind, but they were very vague. I decided to find out from him as much as I could about that old manuscript. He wouldn't answer all my questions, but he did answer some of them. One question he did answer was this: who wrote that old manuscript?"

"Oh, right," said Rachel. "That reminds me: the writer doesn't tell who he is, but he does tell that he wrote from Leyland in 1171. And Mr. Tome said that the ghost who haunts his shop is..."

"William of Leyland," said Joshua, Rachel, and Father Lewis together.

"And Ms. Track mentioned William of Leyland, too," added Rachel.

"She must have got that name from Old Cass," said Father Lewis. "And she did read *The Nicholas Book* a year or so ago."

"But who *is* William of Leyland?" asked Mom.

"I don't know," said Father Lewis, "except that he was a priest in the twelfth century who, according to Old Cass, wrote this brief account of the life of Saint Nicholas."

"But why should he haunt an American bookstore seven hundred and fifty years or more after his death?" asked Dad.

"The connection is the manuscript he wrote, which—and this startled me, as you might imagine, but this is what he said—that manuscript *is* in that American bookstore."

"What?" cried several voices at once.

"That's what he said," replied Father Lewis. "The manuscript, he said, is somewhere in The Old Page Bookshop, though even he does not know where."

"How does he know that?"

The priest shook his head and chuckled. "I do not know," he said. "But according to Old Cass, it is there, somewhere, and it is because of that old manuscript that its author, William of Leyland, can sometimes be seen, haunting the place where the manuscript is hidden. I called Ezra after Old Cass left, and he told me that the ghost is always heard, or, more rarely, appears, during Advent and Christmas, and always for the first time on the sixth of December."

"Why then?" asked Joshua.

"December sixth is the feast day of St. Nicholas," said Dad.

"Correct," said Father Lewis.

"My question," said Dad, "is why a Christian ghost is haunting any place—except Heaven." He spoke carefully, for this was a point of theological disagreement between him and his old mentor, and between their respective church communions.

"According to Old Cass," said the priest, "William of Leyland, as part of the Communion of the Saints, the Cloud of Witnesses, has been given the task—the pleasant task, he says—of returning each year to the place where his manuscript resides, there to read and write of more Heavenly matters."

"But why?" said Rachel.

"He was set this task by Cassiel the angel, to help protect the manuscript. Few mortals will venture to steal a ghost-guarded book."

"But," said Joshua, "how does Old Cass know these things?"

"I don't know," said Father Lewis. "Perhaps even *he* doesn't know how he knows them. And so I cannot say whether he is Cassiel, or whether Professor Princeton is Old Nick. But I do believe there is something strange, something more than meets the eye, about all this." They all fell silent for a few minutes, the only sound the clinking of plates and glasses, and the soft chatter of the younger children.

"There's just one other thing I want to know," said Joshua at last. "What about Santa Claus? Maybe we don't really know if what happened to us today was part of the legend come to life. Maybe we'll never know that for sure. But the whole reason we started our Quest was because we wanted to know the truth about Santa."

Father Lewis glanced at Dad and Mom. "Perhaps this is where you two take over?"

"Yes, I think so," said Dad. He cleared his throat, and was silent for a few moments while he considered how to begin. "I think your confusion about Santa is mostly my fault," he said. "I've never really taught you much about this particular story. Now that I think about it, I believe this is partly because I didn't know how to handle all the competing stories: do I tell you about Rudolph and the North Pole, or do I tell you about the flying sleigh and reindeer? Do I tell you about Nicholas of Myra and the three daughters? Or all of these? Our culture has gotten so mixed up about Santa Claus that I didn't really know how to proceed."

"That's understandable," said Father Lewis.

"But I should have taken the time to figure it out before now," said Dad, "instead of leaving you children at the mercy of pseudo-intellectual bullies like Lou. And I ought to have come to you years ago, Father Lewis, for I can see now that this book of yours would have helped me a great deal."

"And I had no idea you were in doubt on the matter or I should have offered it long ago," replied the priest.

Dad smiled. Then, he took a deep breath and looked at all of them in turn. "So, you want the official word on Santa Claus from Mom and Dad, eh? Well, here it is.

"First, let's deal with your initial question: *is* Santa Claus a real person? I agree with Father Lewis: yes, he is. The Communion of the Saints is real, and we have fellowship, in a mysterious way, with all those who have gone before us, and died, in Christ. And Augustine was right: in one sense, there are no dead. What do the saints who have crossed the firmament into Heaven *do,* now? Certainly they are at rest and peace with our Lord. Do they continue to labor among us? That has been a debate that has divided Christians for centuries."

"Indeed it has," said the Catholic priest with a wry smile.

"Yet this seems to me a somewhat different point," said Dad. "There is no question here of worshiping saints, however that is defined, or of praying to them And let me be clear that there is to be *no* praying to Saint Nicholas in this family, nor writing letters to him, which is just another kind of praying. I suspect that if Nicholas wants to give someone a gift, he can find out what they need, or give them what he thinks best. The only question is whether, under God, the Christian dead may come into this world and serve God. The answer to that is, without doubt, *yes*."

Father Lewis' eyebrows went up. "I'm a little surprised to hear you say that, Joseph," he said. "But carry on."

"Well," continued Dad, "consider Moses and Elijah on the Mount of Transfiguration. These men had either died or, as in the case of Elijah, were in some sense taken to God out of this world. Yet they came back. Perhaps that day on the mountain was not the first time they had returned to the world? Or the last? I don't know, of course. But what Jacob Reuel's book suggests about Saint Nicholas is not so different from Moses and Elijah. In fact, William of Leyland's account says the event of Nicholas's calling was something like what happened to *Enoch* and Elijah. So there is nothing illogical or irrational—or unbiblical—about the idea that Nicholas might have been given a role to play in this world long after he died, or should have died, by human standards."

"But does that mean that he really *was* given such work in the world?" asked Mom.

"Ah, there we enter into the realm of Legend and Mystery," said Dad. "There are more things in Heaven—*and Earth*—than are dreamt of in *my* philosophy. But leave that aside for the moment. I will say this: the story Joshua read today, from Jacob Reuel's book, was the most interesting and compelling story I have ever heard about Santa Claus. It has the ring of truth to it, if you see what I mean, unlike many of the newer, sillier stories. But as Father Lewis said, we cannot know for certain whether it is true. Santa Claus, I know, is not a rosy-cheeked fat man with an addiction to cookies."

"No, *The Nicholas Book* was clear on that point," said Rachel. "But that brings up another question: if the book is true, then does that mean that every time we see a Santa Claus in a department store, or the fat Santas in the cartoons, that it's really the evil Old Nick, the servant of Satan?"

"Or someone working for Old Nick?" put in Joshua.

"I don't know that I would go so far," said Dad. "If the book is true, then yes, Old Nick may have created the Santa Claus of popular books and movies and Christmas songs. But those actors who dress up as Santa and receive visits from children in stores are probably not deliberately working for the enemies of Christ. It may be that they don't know any better."

"And they may themselves be much nobler than that," said Mom. "I remember one Santa at a store when I was a little girl. Even though I only got to talk to him for a few minutes each year, I still remember him as one of the kindest men I ever met. One thing I liked about him was that he never asked me if I had been good. He just asked me if there was a present I would particularly like to have. Gifts were true graces to him, I think, not earned by trying to be extra good for a few weeks every December. He always told me to look for ways to do special things for others during Christmas, and not to think so much about presents. He even told me that the only reason he gave presents to people was to remind them that God had given Himself to us in a manger in Bethlehem. I always wondered whether he was the real Santa Claus: I knew of course that Santa couldn't be in every department store in America at once; but it was enough for me to think that he might have been in *that* one."

"Marian is right," said Father Lewis. "If Grandpa Jacob's little book is true, then of course it's possible that Saint Nicholas just might show up in a department store every now and then, just to see what he can see. Just because Wiseman's Santa has a fake beard doesn't mean there are no *real* beards in the world."

"No," said Rachel, "but it also doesn't mean that every real beard belongs to Saint Nicholas."

"True," answered the priest. "Which brings us back to what your father was saying: if the real Saint Nicholas, today, is not the ho-ho-ho-ing secular god of the modern child, then who is he?"

"He is a servant of Christ who teaches us all what it means to give our lives for others, to sacrifice and bring joy," answered Dad, his eyes narrowing, and his voice taking on an edge of certainty it had not had even a few moments before. "How he does it, I do not claim to know for certain, but he *does*. The proof of this is that we are sitting here talking about him in this way sixteen hundred years after he died, or supposedly died. So let me offer this: how do you know when Nicholas, servant of Christ, has been at work? When you are reminded to help someone in need. When you unexpectedly learn of some way you can bring goodness, truth, beauty, or light to someone's life. When you learn what it means to 'bear one another's burdens.' When you are in despair, and help arrives mysteriously...'how can they have known?' you think to yourself. When you give and receive gifts, whether food, or toys, or treasure, or time. And when your heart has been turned away from the false Santas to Jesus. When these things happen, *Christ* has been at work, in some mysterious way, through His servant, Saint Nicholas, the most powerful symbol of gift-giving in the world. Is there magic involved in all this? You'd better believe it. Which brings us to the point, I think: what really happens on Christmas Eve?"

The children leaned forward in their chairs, their eyes fixed on their Father. This was what they had set out to discover, after all.

Dad spoke in a quieter, but firmer voice. "What happens on Christmas Eve night is mysterious, cloaked in legend. Millions believe that Santa Claus comes to their houses and leaves gifts for children, and for grownups, to remind us of God's gifts to us: the gift of life, and the world, and the Church, and our families, and toys, and food, and books, and salvation itself—God's own Son. What *really* happens on Christmas Eve? I do not claim to know everything. But I do know this: Christmas Eve is the night wherein our Savior's birth is celebrated. It is a gracious, hallowed, holy time. There is wonder in the air, and mystery, and magic. And every Christmas morning, there are always presents there, where there were no presents before—always. And I know for a fact there is a great deal of magic in that." He fell silent, picked up his pipe from the table, and lit it.

Joshua and Rachel were also silent, considering all they had heard this day. Dad's eyes were turned down, but Mom was still looking at her two oldest children, and would have given a truckload of pennies for their thoughts. But she decided it was best to wait.

Father Lewis leaned forward in his chair with a great smile on his face. Then he pointed a forkful of eggs at the children. "It's all in Chesterton, you know. What *do* they teach them in these schools?"

Chapter Twenty

Good Night

After Supper, some more good conversation, and a bit of impromptu Christmas music on Father Lewis' mouth organ (without which he was never to be found), everyone sat around the fire telling jokes and old stories. The younger children were in bed, and it was nearly time for the older siblings to join them.

"You know, I almost forgot one other thing I wanted to show you," said Father Lewis, pulling a small paper item out of his coat pocket. "After Old Cass left this afternoon, I remembered that this was not the first time someone had attempted to steal the book, or part of the book, anyway."

"*Part* of it?" asked Joshua.

"About a year ago, Old Cass told me that he had noticed something about *The Nicholas Book:* something had been taken out of it."

"Taken *out* of it?" said Rachel.

"Yes. After writing his story, Grandpa Jacob had apparently remembered something he had meant to tell. So he wrote a short note, and put it into this small envelope, and tucked it into the final pages of the book." He pulled out the note and read it aloud:

In writing my story, I neglected to mention one little gift that Mr. Nicholas gave me after telling me his story. I enclose it here: it is a gold coin of Roman minting, one of the very coins he had originally given to the three endangered daughters in Myra. It had been passed down through that first father's generations for more than four hundred years until, one day, a distant descendant of that man met Nicholas, many hundreds of miles from Myra. He was the last of his line, and had no children; therefore, he begged

Nicholas to receive back this coin as a token of the gratitude of his family that had never been forgotten through so many generations. And Mr. Nicholas accepted it, but gave it to me, centuries later, on that night of magic. I wish I had the strength to write the story he told me about it, so that you will understand why he gave it to me. Only one other person knows that story now.

"But," said Father Lewis, "I do not know who that one other person is. It was this coin that was stolen from the book. Or perhaps lost, I thought, but Old Cass felt certain that it had been taken. So I took the envelope and note out of the book, since the coin was no longer there."

Joshua and Rachel glanced at each other curiously before Rachel spoke. "Father Lewis," she said, "was there anything...different about this coin? I mean, an unusual mark, for instance."

The priest looked at her with wonder in his eyes. "Yes, there was indeed. The coin had one distinguishing characteristic: a small hole through the middle, just as if it had once borne the mark of a nail. How did you know?"

The children nodded to each other in silent accord. Then Joshua removed from his pocket the little gold coin given them by Ms. Track that morning.

"Here," he said. "We were given this, and asked to give it to you, once our quest was over. We forgot to mention it when we told our story earlier." He told them how they had obtained the coin.

Father Lewis was astonished at the return of the coin. "Yes, this is certainly it," he said. "I suppose Ms. Track couldn't resist a coin once owned by Santa Claus. You know how she is about lucky coins, and all."

"I can't imagine her doing such a thing," said Mom.

"Ah, but strong superstition compels one to do all sorts of bad things. Just think about Lou. Still, she gave it to you children to return to me, so perhaps her conscience got the best of her? But it makes a fine Christmas present to have this returned, and—bless me, I almost forgot!" he added suddenly. Then the kindly priest made his way to the door.

"Be right back!" He ran out to his car, then returned bearing a large, square, mostly flat package, wrapped in tinselly paper with a bow on it.

"My Christmas present for all of you," he said.

Dad and Mom thought Joshua and Rachel should open the present, and so they did.

"Look!" said Joshua as he and the others stared at the gift open-mouthed.

There before them was a large, golden-framed portrait of Saint Nicholas, the same picture they had seen in the back of the book.

"Not the original, which I have at home," said Father Lewis. "But I had several copies made a few years ago, after I found *The Nicholas Book*. That book solved an old family mystery: who was the strange, red-cloaked man in that portrait of Grandpa Jacob's? He never told us, but after reading his book, I knew, of course. I thought maybe this would help you remember the Nicholas of history, the Nicholas who fought to make sure Christ is honored above all else."

"So that part of the story was true at least. Thank you so much!" said Rachel and everyone else spoke words of gratitude to their friend. Father Lewis glanced outside. "Snow's stopped," he said. "Well, I must be going. Thank you for a delightful evening. It is always a true pleasure to see you all. And for you two, my young adventurers, I have one final word: belief in anything, even in your own existence, is always, in some sense, a choice. If we could answer every question, there would be no need for faith. I am certain that this world is magical beyond imagination, if only we could see it. And I am just as certain that Christ lives. As for the rest...well, I am content to live with a little mystery in my life. Maybe this Saint Nicholas book is true; maybe not. But I know what *is* true: God came down to us, and became a human baby in Mary's womb. And with that, let me offer you best wishes for a Merry Christmas! Good night!"

***

Two other things should be mentioned before we end our story. The children went to visit Ms. Track a few days before Christmas, and brought her presents, food, and money (from Mr. and Mrs. Kirk). But the best gift they gave her, in Ms. Track's opinion, was their time. Joshua and Rachel began to visit her once or twice a month, and continued this for more than a year. Ms. Track became a happier sort of person during these years, and while she never taught school again, she did marry a couple of years later and had two children whom she devotedly taught at home, becoming one of the very first modern homeschooling mothers. And a few months after Joshua and Rachel first visited her, she came to church with them. Then one day, about a year later, she actually showed up in church without her lucky necklace.

The other thing is this: two days after the adventure in The Old Page Bookshop, the employees of the Wiseman's Department Store arrived at work to find that, during the night, someone had vandalized the Christmas Kingdom where Santa held court. All the plastic candy canes were broken, the decorations torn down, the fake snow scattered, and the great throne itself literally chopped into pieces. There seemed to be no clue as to who had done it or why, and nothing had been stolen. But it was believed to be an "inside job," since only an employee, one with access to a key, could have gotten inside without breaking a window or door. It took the cleanup crew all day to get the mess cleared away, and another two days to get a new setup for Santa. But later that first day, Joshua and Rachel came by on a hunch, and looked around. Under the wreck of the throne, they found a small Anti-Superstition League button with the letters "L.N." written on the back.

Of course, that didn't prove that Lou had done it. But it is a fact that Lou quit his job that same day, and was never seen in Wiseman's again. No one at the store or among the police made the connection, and if Lou was the vandal, he got away clean.

After finding the ASL button, Joshua and Rachel left, but they came back later in the day. Upon the ruined throne they placed a life-size figure of a baby in a manger, carved from wood and beautifully painted. They had gotten it from a friend of Father Lewis's, who gave it to them for free when he learned what they wanted to do with it. The children did not believe the store would let it stay there for long, but to their surprise, no one touched it for the three days it took to clean up, and rebuild.

In the midst of this crisis, Mr. Wiseman himself, owner of the store, arrived. He was deeply concerned about the vandalism, and especially the effect this might have on business. Yet when he saw the manger, sitting, almost regally, as he thought, atop the broken Santa-throne, he seemed moved. He consulted with his management staff, and together they decided to replace the Christmas Kingdom with a more modest setup. In addition to the more traditional North Pole things, he had Nativity decorations placed all around, with Joshua and Rachel's wooden manger centrally located, and began to play more Christmas carols and hymns, and fewer modern Christmas songs, in his store. He even hired a retired Baptist preacher to play Santa Claus beginning the next year, and encouraged him to talk to the children more about Bethlehem than about baby dolls and baseball bats. Indeed, Mr. Wiseman went so far as to publicly thank the vandal who had torn down his Christmas Kingdom, as well as whoever put the manger on the throne, for bringing about a rebirth of the true Christmas spirit at Wiseman's.

Soon after this, Lou and his family moved away, and his father, in one final shot at his enemies, wrote a guest editorial in *The Skeptic,* which was the "progressive" newspaper in town (too progressive to ever get more than a handful of subscribers), in which he aimed verbal blows at Father Lewis, Ezra Tome, and several others around town, and announced that he was disbanding the Anti-Superstition League, and going off to start a similar group elsewhere, since, as he put it, "Bethlehem is too backwards and superstitious to ever be a center for forward thinking and progress."

***

On Christmas Eve night, Joshua sat in his bed, staring out the window, his arms around his knees. Everyone was in bed, and it was rather late. The sky was completely free of clouds, and it looked as though several million new stars had been quietly added to the firmament. A light snow was falling, and the world had succumbed to that enchanting quietness that comes in with snow.

Joshua heard a slight noise at his door and looked up. Rachel was there, and, when she saw that he was awake, she came and sat down on the bed beside him.

"Well," she said. "Merry Christmas."

"Merry Christmas. I didn't know anyone was still awake."

"I couldn't sleep. I wondered if you had the same problem."

"Yeah. But not a problem, really. I just don't feel tired. I guess I will later, though."

"Joshua," she said. "We haven't really talked much about everything that happened at The Old Page. Not since the night Father Lewis was here."

Joshua looked back out at the snow-world on the other side of his window. "Ever since that night," he said, "I've felt...I don't know, different, somehow."

"What do you mean?" Her voice was intense with curiosity, for she had come precisely for a bit of note-comparing.

"Well," Joshua said, "when we came into the house that night, after getting the tree, I felt like we had gone through a door into another world."

Rachel's eyes flashed with excitement as he said this. "Yes," she said, "that's exactly how I felt! Still do."

Joshua nodded. "It's just the same old house, but... everything about it feels changed. Or maybe...maybe it's..."

Rachel finished the thought. "Maybe it's you—us—that's changed."

"Right."

"It's like we've really lived in Faerie Land all along and didn't realize it. The other day, when you were outside, Dad read me some of the stuff from Chesterton that Father Lewis was talking about. And it's just the sort of thing we kept hearing that day when we had our adventure."

"Like what?"

"Like, why does a tree grow fruit? There's no logical reason why it should. So why does it? Because it's *enchanted*. It's a *magic* tree."

"Yeah, that's the kind of thing I've been thinking about lately. Think about this: right in the next room there are two little people, like us, but smaller: like hobbits or something."

Rachel giggled. "You mean John and Anna."

"Right! But listen: why are they here? Why are *we* here? The same reason: they came *from their mother*, from a whole other person. That's really crazy, when you stop to think about it."

"Yeah, like Dad says, it's not just a story made up for children. But really, it's a much wilder story than the whole stork thing."

"I know! And then there are two other people down the hall: Mom and Dad. Why are they there? Didn't have to be that way. Why does Dad read to us and play with us?"

"And why does Mom make the best cupcakes in the world?"

"Exactly. None of this *had* to happen. And...it doesn't always." He stopped, for this part had also brought him up short in his own private thoughts. In particular, he kept thinking of a boy at school, Bobby Starling, whose father had died at the beginning of the year. How did the magic work for someone like Bobby, whose struggling mother could barely afford Christmas presents? Since that day at The Old Page, Bobby had been much on Joshua's mind, and he had made a few halting efforts at establishing a friendship with the boy, including buying him a Christmas gift. He resolved to do more; but he had come to understand that Bobby's story did not disprove the magic, any more than a shadow disproves the Sun; for without the Sun, there could be no shadow. Instead, Bobby's story reminded Joshua that the gifts in his life were precious, and, in this world, temporary. The knowledge kindled a new fire of gratitude in his awakening heart.

That fire kept Joshua silent for a few moments, before he continued. "I just...felt more excited when we got home that night than I ever felt going to the store to see Santa. I don't know why."

Rachel smiled, and the two of them watched the snow fall for a while. "You know, Joshua," she said, "I'm still not sure about everything—I mean about everything we read in the Old Page Bookshop that day—but I think I'm okay with a little mystery. I don't *have* to know everything."

"Me either. But God really did come to earth as a baby."

"And there really will be presents under the tree in the morning." She sighed and spoke once more in a happy whisper. "And... *The Nicholas Book* just might be true!"

Gratitude

To Angela, for talking and wondering.
To Grace, William, Nathanael, and Abigail, for listening.
To Kaitlyn, for smiling.
To Mom, for reading and correcting.
To G. K. Chesterton, for writing.

Author

William Chad Newsom and his wife Angela are in their twenty-fourth year of marriage, and they are the parents of six home-educated children: Grace, William, Nathanael, Abigail, Kaitlyn, and Sarah, with whom they wrote, produced, and performed an original, three-past audio drama, *The Second Kingdom Book I: A Christmas Mystery*. He is the author of *The Crown of Fire* (historical novel for young readers), *Talking of Dragons: the Children's Books of J.R.R. Tolkien and C.S. Lewis* (literary study for families), and *Family Lore: Kindling a Love of Story in Children*. He has contributed to several volumes of the *Omnibus* curriculum series, published by Veritas Press, and writes and edits for Cross and Quill Media, which provides video and audio reviews for families, along with recommendations for videos and audios to supplement homeschool curricula.

Visit him online at
crossandquillmedia.com
audioadventures.org
or
williamchadnewsom.com

Made in the USA
Las Vegas, NV
21 December 2022

63819609R00089